the

HOMESICK

garden

Kate Cruise O'Brien was born in Dublin in 1948. She is the author of the short story collection, *A Gift Horse*, which won the Rooney Prize. "Henry Died", from this collection, also won the Hennessy Award. She worked with Poolbeg Press as Editor from 1993 to 1998.

the
HOMESICK
garden

Kate Cruise O'Brien

POOLBEG

First published 1991
by Poolbeg Press Ltd
123 Baldoyle Industrial Estate
Dublin 13, Ireland
This edition published 1999
Reprinted March 2000

The Arts Council
An Chomhairle Ealaíon
A catalogue record for this book is available from the British Library.

ISBN 1 85371 144 6

Cover design by Splash
Printed by The Guernsey Press Ltd,
Vale, Guernsey, Channel Islands.

www.poolbeg.com

For Joseph and Alexander, with love

Praise for The Homesick Garden

"*Quite entrancing . . .* "
CYRIL CUSACK

"*I've only read it once and that's not enough for a novel
of this sophistication, it's a wonderful book*"
AUGUSTINE MARTIN

"*Kate Cruise O'Brien has returned, not with a whimper,
but with a bang*"
SUNDAY PRESS

"*. . . a whimsical, sentimental but agonised view of the
world through a child's eye . . .* "
OBSERVER

CHAPTER ONE

Aunt Grace came in out of the rain shivering, trembling and sneezing like a wet dog. It was Sunday morning in our house—everywhere else too, I suppose—but Sunday morning in our house is not the time to pay a call. They were in bed. Dad in the big, bare front room and Mum in the small, squashed back room. They had had a quarrel. They usually do quarrel on Saturday night. There was a lot of door-slamming and talk about drinking (Mum's) and indifference (Dad's) and when I passed Mum on the stairs she was crying but I noticed she had a small glass in one hand and her cigarettes and lighter in the other. I didn't go into the kitchen where Dad was, because I knew he'd just point a finger at me and say "Out" in that tight voice he has. So Dad stayed up late and read the papers at the kitchen table and Mum went to bed early with the brandy and the fags and a big pile of books she used to read when she was a girl. "When I was a girl like you," she said once with a smile. "Only I never was a girl like you. I was something between a coward and a goody-goody and I still read books that are safe and small. It's comforting." Mum needs a lot of comfort one way or another, what with the cigarettes and the brandy and the books but then, I'm not afraid of Dad's tight voice and Mum is. So Saturday night is the reason that no one in their senses would care to call at my house on a Sunday morning and Aunt Grace has a lot of sense. Aunt Grace is my best friend and mentor.

"It's Sunday morning, Aunt Grace," I said as she squelched across the hall. "They're still in bed."

"I'll wait till they get up then," said Aunt Grace. "I've something to tell them and I wanted to be in a house."

"Oh," I said, though I didn't understand in the very least. Aunt Grace has a small untidy flat and usually she hates houses because they have roofs which have to be mended, "And neighbours with noses and dogs," she says. Still there was no point in asking why Aunt G had suddenly developed a liking for houses. You never find out things by asking adults about them. Adults are usually ashamed of wanting to tell. But if you wait long enough they stop being ashamed and get bored at your lack of interest instead. They'll tell you anything if they're afraid you don't want to know about it.

"When did they go to bed?" asked Aunt Grace, who was busy filling up Dad's designer kettle. This was most unlike her. She's not the sort to make herself at home in other people's houses. She might be family and in and out a lot of the time but she's always careful to behave like a guest.

"She went to bed early. He went to bed late," I said. "And I'm not waking them up." I liked it when they were in bed before they'd had time to scratch the house and make it cross. I liked the house silent and calm and bare without the angry little noises made by two people disliking each other.

"You can't be pregnant!" said Mum an hour later. She was standing in the kitchen in her bare feet. She was wearing her old towelling dressing-gown with the tear in the left sleeve. Though Mum can be very elegant during the day it usually wears out by evening and her night clothes would give anyone a headache. Not that I think she should be vampish and sexy for dear old Dad but there are limits. Mum was wearing a short nightie under the dressing-gown. She looked tired and small and shaky.

Grace shrugged. "Well I am, you know, and don't tell me I'm not married because I know that too."

"I wasn't going to say that," said Mum, smiling suddenly, "I was going to say, I don't know what to say. You're so independent. I mean having a baby isn't like you."

"I don't suppose having a baby is like anybody much," said Grace.

"No, that's true," said Mum, forking about in her pocket for her cigarettes, "It's a most unreal thing to do. Are you pleased?" Mum looking pleading. I never knew anyone who wanted people to be happy as much as Mum does. As far as I can tell she's unhappy herself for most of the time but she never seems to give up expecting happiness for herself and for other people. It's as if there's this happy place quite near and Mum knows where it is and what it's like but she just can't get into it, quite yet. You feel she thinks she'll get there quite soon. She's waiting all the time, waiting and wasting her life waiting.

"I'm pleased," said Grace. "I'm pleased and proud and frightened to death and I didn't try to find out about it until now because I was afraid if I gave myself a choice, I'd have to choose."

"How long?" asked Mum who had found her fags and was busy trying to light the cork end of one.

"Wrong end," I said and Mum turned it round, looked disgustedly at the mini-crater in the cork tip and threw it into the sani-can.

"How long? Three months, the doctor said," said Aunt Grace. "But she was cross because I hadn't kept a diary with times of cycles and things. Does she really think I'm going to write that kind of disgusting garbage in my good diary? Besides I didn't quite mean to get pregnant. Anyway it's too late for choices, if that's what you're thinking."

"I wasn't," said Mum vaguely, her mind clearly on other things. "You don't look pregnant, you know. When I was three months I swole up like a balloon."

"Bliss, was it?" asked Aunt G, looking a little less savage.

"Not bliss, exactly," said Mum. "Much better to look back on than I think it was at the time. But it was exciting, even getting fat."

I looked at Aunt Grace. She didn't look fat. Just bulky, no shape at all. She was wearing her usual layers. Damp coat over bulky Aran sweater over shirt, several scarves and a pair of outsize jeans. Aunt Grace is tall, unlike Mum who is short and stocky. Mum worries about her figure all the time—well so does Dad (worry about Mum's figure I mean) but Aunt Grace never does. She just loses her shape in draperies.

"I'm glad about the baby," said Mum squeezing Aunt Grace's shoulder, but this was a mistake because Grace hunched and shied away. She hates being touched. I wouldn't have tried it but poor Mum is a great role player and sometimes she forgets who's who in the dramatis personae of her life. Mum was now the sympathetic sister and she'd forgotten that Grace was not the sort of sister who wanted sympathy.

Mum stopped being sympathetic as soon as Dad came down. Dad was dressed. He does have a dressing-gown but he never wears it. He doesn't even answer the door in an emergency unless he's shaved and has his socks on, armed to meet the world. He must have heard Grace and wondered about her from upstairs but God forbid that he should hurry down—even though he likes her. Sometimes I think he likes her better than he likes Mum. He always offers Aunt Grace another glass of wine even if she's tipsy. If it's Mum, he carefully corks the bottle and glares.

"You offered Grace another glass of wine," said Mum in a fury once. "And she was drunker than I was!"

"Grace is not my responsibility," said Dad in his most pompous voice. Dad is always pompous when he's nervous. "You are my wife and therefore my responsibility." Perhaps Dad would like Mum more if he wasn't married to her.

Anyway Dad came down, trim, slim and brimming with curiosity.

"This is early for a call, Grace?" he said, question-marks fairly bristling from every word.

"It's not a call," said Aunt Grace. "It's an announcement. I'm pregnant and I'm going to have a baby in six months time, and no, I'm not going to tell you who the father is, and I'm very, very happy about it and no, I'm not married."

This all sounded a bit corny to me, even when Aunt Grace put her head down on the kitchen table and howled. I mean no one was blaming her, were they? Mum had been nice. Dad, I could just tell, was about to be very nice and Grace wanted the baby, she said, so what was the big tragedy about?

Mum stood still in her elderly towelling gown looking white and dragging in her lower lip the way she does when she's frightened. Dad put his arm around Aunt Grace in a hearty, awkward sort of way, as if her body wasn't really near his but some way off. It was a very spiritual hug.

"I'm sorry," said Aunt Grace. "It's just that I didn't sleep last night. I guessed I was pregnant, of course, but I didn't really know until the doctor told me and I'd had the test."

"You can get kits from the chemists these days," said Mum. "And do the test yourself. You don't need a doctor to tell you."

She was wandering about, wiping the kitchen counter, clattering a pan, drying a spoon that hadn't been washed. She didn't look at either of them. She was, I knew, very, very, angry.

"You see, I'm not sure I want to be pregnant," said Aunt Grace, looking up at Dad. "I thought I was sure before I knew but now that I know I am, I'm frightened."

"That's very natural," said Dad (how would he know about it?), patting at Grace's shoulder in a timid, repetitive way. "Elizabeth was frightened when she was expecting Antonia, weren't you, Liz?"

"Was I?" asked Mum, pulling the plug in the basin so all the water sucked out in a noisy whirl.

The next morning it was as if Aunt Grace and her pregnancy had never been. It was a freshen-up-for-autumn-all-change-here kind of morning. Mum had ordered both the window-cleaners and the Mini-Maids so the day began at dawn (for us) with much clattering, banging and resentment. Dad hates people working for him. I can understand that. It's hard to watch a frail old man cleaning a window— and all Mum's window-cleaners are old and frail. As for the Mini-Maids, they're holy terrors, not a bit frail or elderly but brisk and young and confident. They bring their own hoovers and dusters and hate my doll collection because I won't let them disturb even one porcelain lady. I know, I know, there is dust in the folds of all their dresses, even Dragon Lady, and they'd look better if they were smartened up but I like them dusty and I can't bear the idea of anyone else touching them or moving them. Mum says I'd clean them myself if I really loved them and that it's frustrating for the Mini-Maids not to be able to clean my room. But I've kind of left the dolls behind. I don't want to clean them in case the magic is gone but I don't want to throw them out or give them to anyone else either, because they were always there.

Dad is never very clear about why he can't put up with the Mini-Maids but he can't. The MMs come every fortnight at eleven o'clock and every fortnight at ten o'clock Mum and Dad have a row. This morning Mum went running early. She runs every day, not very fast, in fact she's always getting upset about her time.

"Twenty-three minutes!" she'll say with one of her mad despairing smiles. "I'm not fit!" Well she isn't, terribly, but what can you expect at forty?

"You might try to enjoy it," I said once.

"Oh darling, I do enjoy it, I just want to be able to do it better."

Quite mad.

Anyway Mum had had her run, she had her shower. She was having her coffee when there was a roar from upstairs.

"What's wrong?" shouted Mum going pale.

"The drawers!" shouted Dad downwards, "Can you never...Oh never mind!"

Mum was furious. "What about the drawers, darling?" she asked, thumping up the stairs in a whirl.

"The point about the drawers, darling," said Dad—actually he was roaring but I knew that he thought he was speaking in a calm and reasonable voice—"is that they're open. The bloody drawers are open and your underwear is spilling out. It's like this every week."

"Every fortnight," said Mum briskly, "Every fortnight, you try something, anything to stop the Mini-Maids coming here. If you don't like it, try closing the drawers!" she screamed. "Try doing the lousy washing-up!"

"Well, your washing-up is lousy," said Dad.

It was silly really, silly if it hadn't been so horrible. Mum's washing-up *is* lousy but then Dad doesn't have much right to talk about it since he never, ever lifts a hand to help Mum. He does do things in the house. He mends it constantly. Roofs and walls and windows. All the things that Mum (and Aunt Grace) hate. But he says Mum doesn't appreciate his efforts in the house, "Doesn't even notice," he mutters, when even a blind fool could see that he just takes Mum's efforts for granted.

Mum came downstairs and tried to put yellow eye-shadow on her red eyes. The effect was bizarre. She was still crying as she stood there at the mirror in the corner of the kitchen, wincing and blinking and stabbing at her poor eyes with a little brush. I didn't say anything because I knew she knew I knew she was crying but didn't want to admit she knew. If no-one said she was crying then she could pretend she wasn't. And why should she care what Dad thinks of her lousy washing-up? I think she gets upset because somewhere, deep down, Mum really does think she's disgusting.

Once, when our cat was dying, I took the laundry to the launderette. Mum didn't know that the cat had got into the laundry basket (for comfort) and been sick in various ways all over it. The launderette returned part of the laundry in a separate bag with a note on it. "The staff at our launderette are not prepared to process these items." When Mum saw the note and the laundry I thought she'd pass out. I thought it was outrageous of them but Mum said no, nobody should have to clean up after the disgusting habits of other, richer people. "You're never paid to hold your nose," she said.

"Were you?" I asked because I remembered the months Mum had spent being "a treasure," a sort of housekeeper in the house of these people she called "The Rich Monkeys."

"No, I wasn't paid for it, but I don't mind blood on underwear or sick on clothes. I don't see it as personal."

Mum put away the eye-shadow and considered the eyeliner.

"No, Mum," I said. "You'll only rub it and get panda eyes."

Mum put down the eyeliner and sighed. "I mean I know I'm a bit messy but I kind of think I've earned it because I don't really mind cleaning up other people's messes. There is blood and shit and vomit and even little babies are nauseating if you don't love them. I just wonder why men think they can escape all that."

We were sitting in the breathlessly tidy kitchen gazing out of the clean windows when Aunt Grace dropped in again. It was a relief really. Mum and Dad hadn't spoken since the Mini-Maids departed and though Dad can be silent quietly, Mum's silences are angry, noisy, clattering affairs.

"Grace!" They both spoke together as if they hadn't seen her for at least six months.

"Grace, do sit down," said Mum.

"Have this chair," said Dad.

"I brought a bottle of wine," said Grace taking a one-and-a-half litre bottle from its wrapping of damp brown paper.

"I'm sorry about yesterday. I was upset."

"That's very natural," said Dad.

"In your condition!" chorused Mum and Aunt Grace together.

"Snap!" said Mum and they both howled with laughter. Suddenly I could see how alike they were.

"I don't see what's so funny," said Dad, trying not to look angry.

"It's not really," said Mum, still giggling.

"Oh it is, it is," said Aunt Grace. "I never thought I'd hear anybody think that about me—'In your condition'!"

They both giggled and giggled. I looked at Dad and Dad looked at me. Clearly demented the pair of them.

The next morning was school, oh dreaded day, and the usual fuss about the alarm clock. We have eight alarm clocks in our house and only one of them works. It's a neat black alarm clock with nothing fancy about it but it does work. It also belongs to Mum. Now Mum is usually very cheery and optimistic about getting up in the morning when it's twelve o'clock at night.

"Of course I will, darling, I always wake up. Besides this term I'm going to write in the mornings so I'll have to wake up."

But in the morning she's growly and cross and, well, to put it bluntly, she doesn't wake up. Dad says she wanders around the house at all hours making coffee and having snacks and reading but at six or so she goes off to bed thinking, no doubt, that she has woken up—and at half seven she's dead to the world. So I wanted the alarm clock.

"But you have your own alarm clock," said Mum. "The clock radio."

"It's broken," I said. "The black clock is the only one that works. Can I have it?"

"But I'll wake you," said Mum. "I always wake up."

"Mum," I said. "You don't always wake up. I was late for school three times last term because you said you always wake up and quite frankly you don't."

I thought that sounded priggish. Mum thought so too.

"Well if you're so perfect," she said furiously, "buy yourself your own bloody alarm clock out of your own money and don't expect me to get up in the morning to see you off because I won't!"

So I took the alarm clock and set it and at ten to eight I woke Mum who was growly and cross and half asleep but she'd quite forgotten about not getting up and not seeing me off. She staggered around in her short nightie and towelling gown but she lit the fire and turned on the radio and you could imagine, if you tried just a little, that we were a normal family. Eating cereal, listening to radio at table in clean kitchen in front of gas fire. Mum even fussed about my reflector belt—on a bright sunny autumn morning!—and told me to ride carefully. She didn't shut the front door until I'd turned the corner. Oh dear.

Do I like school? I don't know really. I remember reading once about a little boy who'd got expelled and he said, "But I can't leave school now. There's so much more of it." That's the way I feel. School is just something you do. It's not horrid or nice. It's just school. I feel slightly homesick there most of the time which is silly because it's only a mile and a half away. I like the work part and I get on quite well with most of the other people in the class but they're not friends really. Sometimes I don't think I really am at school. I'm just visiting and working there. I don't enjoy break or lunch because those are friend-times and not having a friend makes you conspicuous. I work in the library then.

Oddly enough I like the people in my class better when

they are in class. They seem intelligent then, and interesting. But at break and lunch there's a lot of giggling and gossip about boys, boys, boys and I don't have a boyfriend and I don't think I want one either. It's funny. People like Clarinda and Sandra who are great gigglers and boy fanatics never seem to think about what boys mean. They can look very serious in RE class when we discuss marriage but they never seem to connect that with giggling about boys.

I will never, ever get married. I'd rather be like Aunt Grace, layers and all, than like Mum, creeping around the house. I hate it when people say "Oh well, she'll change her mind." It's horrid to have your mind taken away from you and arranged by adults.

But riding to school this morning with no homework on my back and the house behind me, I felt much freer and more intelligent than I had for ages. There's something very foggy about the atmosphere at home. I'm just beginning to wonder who is the father of Aunt Grace's baby and what, oh what, is Grandma going to do or think or say? I have a sudden vision of Mum sitting at the kitchen table, laughing.

"Grandma won't do or say anything," says Mum. "Grandma will just forget."

It's all enough to make you cry.

❦❦❦

CHAPTER TWO

My bedroom is beside the front door. Mum said she arranged it that way so that I could come and go without her having to notice too much. "When you get older," she said. Fat chance of Mum not noticing everything. Actually I think she arranged it that way so that I could answer the door when she doesn't want to, which is most of the time. She always seems to live in dread of meeting something unexpectedly nasty on the doorstep. This evening, three weeks after school started, the doorbell rang. Mum was tapping at her typewriter and shouting and tearing paper. Dad was at work. Dad cooks for a living. He's a chef and nothing wrong with that, though Dad seems to think there is. The doorbell rang again. There was a sound of shuffling and stamping in the porch.

"Mum!" I shouted. "I can't answer it. I'm not dressed!"

"Say I'm in the bath!" she shouted back.

"I can't say anything. I told you. I'm undressed."

So Mum came down, tippidy, tappady, polite and happy-sounding on the stairs.

"Good evening," she said.

"Good evening," said a polite male voice.

Silence.

"Can I help you?" said Mum.

"I'm Grace's Brian," said male voice.

"Oh," said Mum hopefully, "are you a Jehovah's Witness?"

Mum likes the Jehovah's Witnesses because they engage her in lively Biblical debates. Mum is a non-believer but she was brought up a Protestant and, she says, she is therefore one of the few people in Ireland who has actually read the Bible.

"Did Grace tell you I was a Jehovah's Witness?" asked the male voice, sounding alarmed.

"I don't know," said Mum, sounding like Grandma in one of her vaguer moods. "Are you collecting? I don't give to the Legion of Mary."

"I'm Grace's Brian," said the male voice. "You know, your sister Grace. Are you your sister Grace's sister?" he asked desperately. "Are you Elizabeth, sister of Grace? Because if you are, I'm Grace's, well, I'm Grace's man."

"Grace's man?" asked Mum sounding astounded. "I didn't know she had a man."

"Well she must have, mustn't she?" said the reasonable male voice which I was hating more every minute. "She must have a man because she's pregnant. I'm the father."

"Whose father?" said Mum.

I was dressed. I just hadn't wanted to answer the door. Like Mum, I thought it was collectors and I never know how to deal with them. I went into the hall and saw that Mum still had the door on the chain. She didn't like Grace's Brian. That much was clear. Mum is very quick-witted until she decides not to be. Then she suffers from something that Dad calls willed amnesia. Like Grandma, who quite simply forgets everything she doesn't want to remember.

"I think Brian is the father of Grace's baby, Mum," I said, pulling her back and undoing the chain. "I think he wants to talk to you."

Grace's Brian was large and wide and handsome. I

detested him on sight. He smelled of aftershave and had that cushiony kind of black hair that sparkles on a rainy night. He wore a Burberry raincoat, which he took off and handed to me without being invited. Underneath the Burberry was a shiny, well faintly shiny, suit, the sort that Dad calls Alumicron. Also a shirt and matching tie. He looked and smelled respectable in a sleazy sort of way. I mean there was something deeply cheap about him. I didn't like the fact of him standing there in our golden yellow hall and I could see that Mum didn't like it either.

"I'm sorry," said Mum, "it's rather late," looking at her watch which wasn't on her wrist. "It's rather late and I'm working. I wasn't expecting anyone...Grace didn't tell me you might call."

Call indeed. Mum could have said that she didn't even know this man existed. Grace hadn't said anything about Brian and if ever, in my wildest dreams, I had tried to imagine a father for Grace's poor baby I wouldn't have had the lurid, bleak sort of imagination that could have conjured up a man like this one. I mean Grace in her layers and this vision of suburban sleaze. "Don't be a snob, Antonia." I could just hear Mum saying that in my head. But Mum didn't like him either. I could see that and hear it and feel it. She was stiff with a kind of raging awkwardness and she was trying to decide, I could tell, whether to invite him into the (cold) dining-room or into the (messy) kitchen.

"Shall we go down?" said Grace's Brian, taking Mum by the arm and leading her towards the kitchen which was the only obvious place you could go to from the hall. Still, you had to hand it to him. Most guests wait to be told where to go and if Grace's Brian had waited he might well have spent the evening standing in the hall listening to Mum dithering.

The kitchen was warm and messy, not very messy but enough to start Mum clattering and cleaning and apologising.

"It's OK," said Grace's Brian.

"Do you want coffee or tea or a drink? We don't keep spirits in the house, I'm afraid," said Mum, sounding Puritan. No indeedy, Mum, we don't keep spirits in the house, we drink them instead.

"Oh, anything," said Brian. I was sure he was longing for a large gin and tonic with lemon and ice. He wasn't a beer sort of man. Too clean, I thought. He was obviously beginning to feel uncomfortable. Perhaps he thought he'd stepped into the wrong house, what with Mum burbling about Jehovah's Witnesses and the Legion of Mary and saying that she didn't keep spirits in the house.

"Perhaps a glass of wine," said Brian hopefully.

"Oh, wine," said Mum as if she'd never heard of the stuff.

"I'll get the wine," I said and picked out the big bottle which Aunt Grace had left three weeks before. Both Mum and Dad said that it was toxic and must have been made from banana skins. So Mum had written Cooking on it in large letters and Dad had said that it should be kept for particularly mean and nasty guests. I turned the label away from Grace's Brian and ignored Mum's wittering about how it wasn't chilled. I found two (reasonably) clean glasses and poured a great slosh into each. And then I waited.

"I did want to talk to you about Grace," said Brian.

"Well go ahead," said Mum, sipping the wine and wincing. I knew she'd rather have beer.

"It's rather private really," said Brian with a nod in my

direction. "Little pitchers."

"I'm sorry. I don't understand you," said Mum.

"Could I talk to you alone?" said Brian.

"Oh, Antonia knows all about Grace's baby," said Mum. "Grace told all of us. She didn't know it had a father, of course. Antonia, I mean. Grace should have told us." Mum looked reproachfully at Brian and I tried not to giggle.

"I knew it wasn't the Immaculate Conception, Mum," I said.

"Yes, well," said Mum. I could see that she was thinking that there was a lot to be said for the Immaculate Conception.

"I'm sure you're very frank with Antonia," said Brian, winking, yes *winking* at me, "but I must confess I'm a bit nervous...I'd rather talk to you alone."

"Oh, in that case," said Mum grandly, and Mum can be very grand indeed, "if you're nervous, I'll tell Antonia to go away but I must tell you that I'll tell her everything you tell me. It's not a matter of principle, you understand. It's just that I always do tell Antonia and I think you'd better know that."

"Oh," said Brian, taken aback. He wanted to talk. He wanted to talk like anything but I could see that he wanted the frills as well. He wanted to have his story—whatever it was—dragged from his unwilling breast. No doubt he'd hoped that he could swear Mum to secrecy and that she'd leak the secrets out in a discreet sort of way that would make him look like A Man Driven to Talk. Perhaps he hoped that he could speak to Grace through Mum. People do that all the time—particularly when they're bad at talking. They tell you something they want you to tell to someone else, as if it's realer and more honest by remote control.

Brian had reckoned without Mum. Mum simply didn't

want to listen to him. If she had wanted to listen to him she'd have got me out of the way immediately. Oh she would have told me what he said but she wouldn't have told him that—or not told him that either. The question wouldn't have come up. It would have been "Out, Antonia!" and I'd have gone.

"Out, Antonia," said Mum now, nodding her head at the door.

"Oh, all right," I said, flouncing and hoping to make Grace's Brian feel bad. I wasn't sorry really. I was sure that Mum's account of what Grace's Brian said would be much more interesting than anything he could manage on his own.

"What did he say, Ma?" I asked when the front door closed two hours later.

"Oh, dear God," said Mum striding towards the kitchen and the beer. "What didn't he say? The man's disgusting, disgusting, disgusting," and Mum opened the fridge door, found the beer, unzipped it and let forth a gust of froth.

"Is he a pervert?" I enquired eagerly.

"How would I know?" snapped Mum. "Or you either. I've never met a pervert and I suspect I wouldn't know one if I saw one. There is something wrong about him. He's all wrong because he's all right—if you see what I mean. He wants to marry Grace."

I did see what she meant. Mum has this bizarre theory that honest men don't want to marry women. She thinks courtship (by men of women) is sinister and that sentimental men who woo women with flowers and like church weddings are hiding something. She's never quite worked out this theory of hers. It just hangs around the edge of her conversation.

"Any decent honest man," she once said to Dad, "would have the courage to admit that he was frightened to death of marriage." It was one of the nicest things I ever heard her say to Dad because she makes it perfectly clear that he didn't want to marry her—at first anyway. She proposed to him and he had to be given time to think it over.

"Well, what did Brian want?" I asked. Mum was twitching about, fiddling, making faces at herself in the mirror, cleaning this and moving that.

"I'm not sure. I think he wanted me to tell Grace to marry him. He wanted me to know that he's not the sort to let a lady down and that he's no male chauvinist pig either. On the other hand he asked me what sort of a future would 'the little lad' have if he was brought up in a household of women."

"What women?" I asked. "I mean there's only Grace."

"Oh I don't know," said Mum. "I may not be being fair to him. He doesn't talk quite like that. I haven't got his voice right yet. But he did say 'little lad.' Why should the child be a little lad? It might well be a little lass. I think he's got a thing about women. I mean no fruit from his loins is going to be raised in enemy territory. From what he said about Grace—and didn't say—I gather he thinks she's the enemy. Woman enemy."

"Dad's not like that," I said. I don't always try to repair my parents' marriage but there are times when I feel the need to put in a word for each of them. It seems strange that two such nice, kind, intelligent and sensible people could possibly make such a mess of their lives. I mean they're not even happy being miserable.

"No," said Mum. "Dad's not like that. I remember when I wanted to have a baby he said that every woman had the right to have at least one baby. He was nervous about it. We were poorish and we didn't have a house. We lived like students and having a baby seemed an unlikely adult sort of thing to do. I mean very few of our friends were even married." Mum sighed. "It seems strange now when teenagers are almost elderly but our friends disapproved of marriage and domesticity—all the sort of things I liked— and having a baby in that kind of atmosphere was difficult. And I used to think that Dad cared too much about what people thought, about what his friends thought. I thought he'd feel uncomfortable stepping out of line. I thought he'd discourage me. But he didn't. In fact," said Mum with a smirk, "he was very pleased about it when I got pregnant, proud of me, you know. He'd walk down the street holding my hand even when I was enormous. It's odd," Mum looked puzzled, "he's so good in some ways."

That's the trouble with trying to get your parents to like each other. They get sentimental instead. Or edgy. By edgy I mean they start edging the conversation towards sex, they start telling you things you don't really want to know. Mum made me feel awkward. I knew there was a time before I was born but I wasn't sure that I wanted to hear about it— that way. In any case I didn't really see why she should feel so grateful to Dad just because he let her have a baby. I was the baby after all. I think he was lucky. But there was no arguing with Mum in this mood. She was wallowing in the past, getting to like Dad fifteen years too late.

"Mum," I said, "I think you should go to bed."

I could feel a storm brewing. Mum was liking Dad, fifteen-years-ago Dad, but the Dad who was going to come through the front door in two hours or so wasn't that Dad at all and Mum wasn't pregnant any more.

"Why not just let them quarrel?" Aunt Grace says when I worry about them. "You can't change them, you know, and they may like quarrelling. You should get on with your life and let them get on with theirs."

Which is all very well, but how can I get on with my life when I spend so much of my time worrying about them? Besides Aunt Grace doesn't think that they'll ever separate and I do. Aunt Grace never hears them fighting in the night—and I do.

Mum didn't go to bed. I did. Dad came home late. There was a murmuring in the kitchen and that night they shared the same bed. That was a week ago. I still haven't got anything out of Mum about beastly Brian or his several sins and Grace hasn't been around once, which is unusual. However this morning, Saturday, we had a visit from Grandma.

Grandma is Mum's mum, though that sounds too cosy a word for her. She's Grace's mum too, of course. Grandma is a small, pretty, seventy-year-old widow with pale hair, neither grey nor gold. She is always elegant in a slightly dated sort of way. Structured somehow. Not a curl nor a curve out of place. She wears a longline corset, one of those ones that has suspenders to hold up stockings and she thinks that both dieting and exercise are "inadequate ways of controlling your figure." Grandma simply locks her body into a ghastly straitjacket so that she can't eat. She claims that she eats "like a bird" and she fusses about her tiny appetite in restaurants.

"I simply can't eat that," she says. "I have a tiny appetite. I eat like a bird." Dad says that some day some waiter will murder her with a carving knife and that she's more like a vulture than any other bird he ever came across. But then

Dad hates Grandma. I once asked him about that when he was angry.

"She has an ugly nature," he said, "which makes other people feel ugly."

"Other people like Mum?" I said.

"Something like that," said Dad. Grandma does make Mum feel ugly.

"Have you put on weight again EEElizabeth?" she'll say and Mum will slouch in her T-shirt and jeans. Mum has a pretty good figure when she sits up straight but something about Grandma's biscuity voice makes her round her shoulders and cringe her arms over her front, defending herself again, poor Mum.

The other thing about Grandma is that she's vague. I don't-quite-mean that she's senile. As I said before, Dad calls it "willed amnesia." Grandma forgets anything and everything she doesn't want to remember.

On this occasion Grandma had forgotten why she had come to call before she got through the front door.

"Grace," she said, shaking her umbrella at the neighbourhood cat who was cowering in the corner of the porch. "Grace, something about Grace, EEElizabeth. I came to talk to you about Grace."

"I'm not Mum," I said. "I'm Antonia." I knew Mum was lurking upstairs.

"Ah, Antonia," said Grandma, looking at me out of her pale blue eyes. "The baby."

It didn't fool me.

"Grandma, I'm fifteen years old."

"You'll soon be older," said Grandma handing me the umbrella. "Look what happened to Grace."

"What did happen to Grace?" I asked. I knew, of course.

I just wanted to know what Grandma was going to admit she knew.

"Pregnant," said Grandma. "Pregnant at her age! The talented one! The bright one! The passionate one! My baby!"

Grandma moved smartly towards the kitchen—not unlike Brian in some ways. She handed me her coat, tut-tutted about "the mess, the mess," and then sat down abruptly at the kitchen table.

"This is making me feel very old, Antonia," she said. "I do not like that man." She looked out at me from those vague blue eyes and I could almost feel sorry for her. She did look shaky and old and she'd remembered my name. But Dad says that Grandma is a dangerous mixture of passion—selfish passion—and cunning and that her likeable moments are her most dangerous ones.

"What man, Grandma?"

"Grace's man. He came to call. He wants to marry her."

"Lots of people get married, Grandma," I said. "William-and-Mary, Queen Victoria, Marie Curie." At least I'd struggled out of English queens in the very nick of time. But not quick enough for Grandma.

"And, what, may I ask, about the Virgin Queen?" declaimed Grandma. "Did she get married? I called EEElizabeth after her you know."

"You got married, Grandma."

"I did. I know," nodded Grandma as if she were making a big concession by admitting something everyone knew, "but that was different."

It's amazing the way people think they are different enough to make bad rules perfect.

"Women did get married in my day," Grandma went on. "You married a foolish husband and hoped to make sense of him. Otherwise," she said, trailing her fingernail across the gritty tablecloth and coming up with a horrid pile of dusty sugary salt, "otherwise you had no power."

It was a long and thoughtful speech for Grandma, perfect widow and martyr. Dad says Grandma was a widow all her life. When Grandpa finally died, Dad says, Grandma came into her reality. But usually Grandma reveres Grandpa's memory. The memory of his death. She can never remember a moment of his active life but she can remember the magic minute when he put his hands to his chest, the long hours in the intensive care unit, the tubes, the machines, the nurses who said how brave she was. Nothing became Grandma so well as Grandpa dying. She thought that each and every funeral wreath—there were a lot—was a personal tribute to her.

"How kind everyone is to me," she used to murmur, her little soft pink cheeks puffing with pleasure. "So very kind."

Mum came down then, slowly. I knew she'd heard Grandma. Our house has the kind of walls that reverberate to a visitor's voice. But Mum, I guessed, had been trying to find her thin clothes. There's no use telling her that if she'd stand up straight and lift her chin and tell the old bat to go to hell she'd feel better—and thinner. Oh no. When Mum hears Grandma's voice she rushes for her size tens. Mum is a size twelve and squeezing only makes her look fatter but I think Mum thinks that the mere fact of a size ten on a label automatically makes her thinner. Mum doesn't know how to be a fine figure of a woman. She only knows how not to be thin.

On this occasion Mum had resurrected a long narrow pencil-line skirt and an even smaller blouse. She'd borrowed Dad's herringbone jacket to hide the gaps but it didn't work. She looked like a fat thin person instead of a medium-sized medium person and she was hunching and cringing as she came through the door.

"EEElizabeth," said Grandma rising and attacking her with kisses. Smack. Smack. On each cheek. "EEElizabeth, why, you look frowsty!" Grandma used the kind of words you only read in books. I keep on wondering whether anyone else ever uses them and if Grandma's pronouncing them right.

"Frowsty," said Mum, scratching her head. "I suppose I do. I'm tired."

"You look tired," said Grandma, without pity.

Mum did look tired. Frail and fat. She always seemed to swell in Grandma's presence.

"Grace," said Grandma, cutting the cackle. "Grace, Grace, I've come about Grace."

"Well, Mother," said Mum who hardly ever calls Grandma Mother, "I didn't think you'd come about me."

"No I didn't," said Grandma. "I gave you up long ago. You got *married*. You were clever and pretty. Your father thought you'd go far. We spent a fortune on your education. It would be worth it, *he* said. But I knew different. You always wanted to please people, to get them to like you. You had no courage, no passion. You couldn't work for yourself. So you married a cook!"

I'd never heard Grandma like this. Oh, Mum and Dad had told me stories but I'd never quite believed them. Dad says that Grandma is always vicious. She just hides it sometimes. Mum looks puzzled and wonders whether Grandma is mad, right or prophetic.

"I never did do very much for myself," Mum will say. "And they did spend a lot on my education."

This morning with the winter light coming through the smeary windows (we needed the window-cleaners again) I thought that Dad was righter than Mum was. Grandma was vicious and it's very easy to sound prophetic and true if you're prepared to be mad enough—and bad enough—to break the rules and hurt people. Frightened people tend to believe vicious ones.

"I don't like that man," said Grandma.

"Grace's Brian?" said Mum. "I don't like him either but it's really none of our business. Grace didn't ask us to like him."

"But she's pregnant!" said Grandma, who always stuck fast to the few facts she could remember. "He wants to marry her! She'll give in, I know. There's no strength or courage in this family! You're all weak, weak like your father was weak. You could have had careers!"

"Grace does have a career, Mum," said Mum.

"AAAUGH!" said Grandma making a sound like a strangled whale. "A career indeed. She's just a schoolteacher. And you, you sit around trying to pretend you're doing something. You say you're writing. Writing indeed. When did you ever publish anything that mattered to anybody?"

Mum, who had looked fairly grey to begin with, now went green. Mum does copywriting for advertising agencies. She's not very good at it, she says, but it pays some bills. She also secretly writes stories. She hides them in my file, "Antonia, School etc." I suppose she thinks that no one will look into that file but I found them one day when I was looking up an old school report to see if I was getting better or worse. Teachers are always saying you're improving or disimproving when you're not. So I like to check. Anyway I found Mum's stories all neatly typed. They're good stories

too. I probably wouldn't have read them if they weren't
secret. If she'd given them to me I'd have tried not to read
them. But since the stories were just there not asking for
attention or anything, I did read them. I never told her I'd
found them or read them. It was as if she was writing secret
letters to me and if I told her I knew, the letters would stop.
Letters from another Mum. Because Mum's stories are a bit
magic and not at all like everyday Mum. They're confident,
straight-backed, brave, not timid at all and yet they're hidden
away in a file marked "Antonia, School etc." I wonder if she
hoped I'd find them.

"You have both wasted your education and your talents,"
said Grandma. "After all I've done for you." Grandma
expects value for money, you see. Come to think of it it
wasn't Grandma's money that paid for the education, it
was Grandpa's. Mum sat clenched at the kitchen table. She
once told me that when she was a little girl she used to
clench her toes so that the sound of her mother's angry
voice wouldn't travel up her ankles to her legs, to her head.

"I used to have those cut-out leather sandals then," she
told me. "And I would watch my brown toes going white."

"Grace has disappeared," said Grandma, looking pathetic
again. "That horrid man came to see me and told me Grace
must marry him. He came at night and I rang Grace and
she didn't answer. I know she was there though." Grandma
looked cunning.

"You can't know that, Mum," said Mum looking upset.
I think she thought that that was just the sort of thing the
old witch would know.

"I *do* then, EEElizabeth," said Grandma. "I feel it *here!*"
And she pressed her bony chest. "But I've called around to
Grace's flat, that horrid flat, and she's not there, or if she

is there she's not answering and I don't have a key. Why didn't she give me a key when I asked her? She isn't at the flat. She isn't at school. She isn't anywhere. I'm so worried, so worried, EEElizabeth. How could she do this to me?"

I could think of a few reasons and as Mum sat there, grey to green and swelling with fear, I'm sure she could think of a few reasons too.

❦❦❦

CHAPTER THREE

G race did not reappear. "I'm sure she'll turn up," said Dad who came downstairs, ever so bravely, after Grandma had left. Mum had to get Grandma a taxi because—fortunately, Dad said—we don't have a car. If we did have a car Mum would spend all her time ferrying Grandma about. Grandma, of course, thinks she's too frail to drive.

Mum rang Grace's flat, no reply, and then she rang Grace's school on Monday but they said she'd been due some leave and had taken it.

"In the middle of the winter term?" asked Mum.

"Sick leave," said the school person.

"You can't be *due* sick leave," said Mum, who is literal minded.

"It depends why you're sick," said the voice at the other end, according to Mum. It sounded a bit deranged so Mum may have invented it. She likes to add a little spice to life.

"We're stuck," said Mum putting down the phone and looking almost happy. "We're stuck. There isn't a thing we can do."

"Not a thing, EEElizabeth," said Dad putting his hands in front of her hunched shoulders and trying to draw them back. "Are you sure, EEElizabeth, that there isn't a rich source of guilt you could tap? Isn't Grace's Brian your fault somehow?"

"Oh shut up!" said Mum, looking even happier.

The thing is, Mum *is* happy now that Grace has, as it were, disgraced herself. Grace has gone and Mum doesn't want to find her. Brian calls around almost every night.

"Where is she?" he asks Mum night after night. "Where is she? Why is she hiding from me?" Mum is too happy to answer. I feel like screaming at her sometimes. It's all right now Mum, you're vindicated. You're the clever one. You might have married a chef—sorry, cook—but you never slept with a man like Brian. Dad, who loves Grace, is very patient with Brian. But then Dad goes out to work at five-thirty and Brian usually arrives at five-fifteen. Fifteen minutes isn't long to be patient in.

The other day Brian came in after Dad had left and said to Mum, "Do you mind if I ask you something, Elizabeth?"

"No," said Mum ambiguously.

"I wonder how many children you have?"

Mum looked around, pointed at me and held up one finger.

"One. One as far as I know. There aren't any others lying about. I've been married once. I have one husband and one child."

"That's strange you know, Elizabeth," said Brian in his odd Australian-American voice (Dad says he's on the run). "That's very strange because your mother keeps saying that you have far too many children. How can that be?"

"You're not Irish, are you Brian?" asked Mum in a quick, angry voice. "I mean I don't quite know *what* you are but you're not born and bred Irish. That's certain. My mother is a strong-minded, unhappy, powerful woman. She thinks she could have been wonderful if she hadn't been burdened by children. She dislikes men, children and sex almost equally. When my mother hears about a birth she counts nine months backwards and is disgusted. Now do you understand? One child is far too many."

"But your mother had two," said Brian, who is a bit slow.

"Yes," said Mum. "And she's never stopped being disgusted. What do you think is wrong with Grace and with me?"

"All I know is that Grace has disappeared," said Brian. He shuffled off then without even finishing his beer. It was a record. He'd turned out to be a beer man after all. Perhaps because there was no gin and less tonic in our house. Mum had been threatening to stock only low-alcohol beers but nothing ever came of that. I don't think she could bear Brian without beer, fairly strong beer, and now she was delighted. She did a merry little tap-dance on the kitchen floor.

"That was cruel," she said, looking triumphant and pleading all at once. "Do you think I was cruel telling him that?"

"I don't know," I said crossly. All I knew was that this was getting too grown-up for me. Edging again. Sex and stuff.

"Mum?" I asked, "don't you ever really wonder where Aunt Grace *is*?"

"Oh I do, I do," said Mum. "But I've wanted to disappear all my life. If Grace has managed it why should I stop her?"

❦

I knew that Grace was in her flat. I knew that better than Grandma did when she pressed her hands to her bony chest. I knew because I knew Grace. I met Grace when I was seven. I'd always known her, aunt, teacher, bored adult, but I didn't really get to know her, meet her, until I was seven years old. Then Mum went off for a week. She wouldn't say where she was going. She'd been doing a lot of crying around that time.

"I can't *cope!*" she would shriek from the kitchen in the night. "I have to go *away!*" The shrieks took my sleep away. I'd count the cars, not many, stopping and starting in the road.

I'd wait for the birds in the morning and the milk-van. It must have been spring or summer because the birds started long before the milk-van. The milk-van was safer. The milk-van chased away the night and the shrieks.

Anyway Mum went. She hugged me very tight and she cried but she went. Grace held my hand as the taxi disappeared down the road.

"Well, let's go," said Aunt Grace.

"*Where* are we going?" I asked.

"We're going," said Aunt Grace looking up at the sky for inspiration, "we're going to my homesick garden. And we'll walk."

We walked. Down by the poor buildings with their tired red-brick fronts which frightened me because the boys from there threw snowballs at me in winter. Besides I didn't like the poor smell and the bony bare look of the open hallways. We went past The Hill pub and down to the canal and over the bridge. We went down the towpath where—Dad had told me—men used to walk beside the barges down the canal.

"Where *is* Dad?" I asked Aunt Grace.

"Busy," said Aunt Grace. "Men are always busy. That's the first rule."

"What's the second rule?" I asked. "What's the second rule, Aunt Grace?"

"Oh *God*!" said Aunt Grace. "The second rule is...the second rule is my homesick garden."

"A garden isn't a rule," I said.

"This one is a rule unto itself," said Aunt Grace crossly, stamping along the towpath. I was getting tired. Aunt Grace walked very fast and she was holding my hand as if it was part of her arm.

"I live surrounded by a homesick garden and in that homesick garden we will imagine three impossibly homesick thoughts before breakfast."

"I've had breakfast, Aunt Grace," I lied. "Mum made it for me before she left." And then I sat down on the grass beside the canal and cried. Aunt Grace had to sit down too because her rapid arm was attached to my hand.

"Oh dear, oh dear," said Aunt Grace. "I'm *sorry*. The funny thing is, I'm homesick too."

"You're too old to be homesick," I said. "You're too old to have a home with parents in it. And you have a flat."

"You're never too old to be homesick and sometimes I think that not having a home is likely to make you more homesick than anything else. I mean, I think you miss the things you don't have much more than you miss the things you do have." She was talking to herself but I didn't mind. It was comforting, like eating when you feel like crying. She made a normal noise and she didn't keep asking me questions. Most adults question you when you cry and get cross when you don't answer. And yet they don't really want you to answer. They just want you to stop crying. So that they'll feel better. Aunt Grace was the first person I had ever come across who was genuinely interested in tears and being homesick. She made me feel as if homesickness wasn't terrible and panicky at all, but fairly usual and real.

Ĩ think I started to love Aunt Grace then. Before that she'd just been an aunt I was supposed to love. So I thought I knew where Aunt Grace was now. Not just because I loved her. In fact I think that love, whatever Grandma says, is just as likely to confuse you as not. People often seem to be frightened of people they love and the fear makes them stupid. Like Mum and Dad. But Grace and I knew each other when we were both unhappy. I don't know why Grace was unhappy then, but she was, and lonely too. We were both lonely together. Lonely and hurt and jagged at the edges. It made us very polite to each other and careful, equal too. That was the astonishing thing. I never thought of Aunt Grace as old again or perhaps I never thought of myself as very young again. In Grace's flat we were like two frail, polite old ladies. In the homesick garden we were like mad children.

Three impossible homesick thoughts before breakfast. Aunt Grace never had breakfast. She was very amateur about adult things.

"Oh dear, no milk, no cereal," she'd say. "I never eat breakfast, you see. There's usually leftovers of a takeaway or something. You don't really want breakfast, do you?"

"Children need breakfast," I'd say and Aunt Grace would laugh and take me to the local shop where we'd buy bread and milk and cereal. I had to tell her which kind. Aunt Grace always said that sandwiches would be simpler because of no dishes and spoons and we could eat them outside but I pointed out that shops didn't have sandwiches ready-made-up in the morning and if they did they'd be stale.

"Sandwiches are for lunch, Aunt Grace. This is ten

o'clock."

"Yes, well," said Aunt Grace, "I don't usually get up at ten o'clock in the holidays." It was the holidays and I'm fairly sure, as I remember that time, that it was summer. Summer in Aunt Grace's little stifling hot kitchen under the roof. The kitchen had a sort of pipe to the roof and when it rained, which wasn't often, the rain came in on our heads. Ventilation, Aunt Grace called it. The bathroom was a room off the kitchen. Quite illegal, Aunt Grace said, but interesting too because when you let the water out of the kitchen sink, tea leaves came up in the bath. Aunt Grace took to buying breakfast the day before. She bought bread and butter and sardines because she didn't like ham and I didn't like cheese and somehow we'd never been allowed enough sardines before. And Aunt Grace made sandwiches after our takeaway in the evening while I lay on the sag bag and listened to her humming along to the music on the crackling radio. Vague, silly music it was too but Aunt Grace said that she hated, really hated, classical music on her own. The radio was much less frightening, she said.

"Radios are for single people who need to know that someone else is alive somewhere," she said. "Classical music is for people who are cosy enough to contemplate tragedy."

Did she say that then? I got to know Aunt Grace so well afterwards that I can never remember which was then, homesick-garden-time, and which came later. Aunt Grace went on being the same and the only thing that changed was the homesick garden. We never used it after that summer.

Aunt Grace's flat was on the top of a tall narrow house near the canal. Dad said that though Dubliners called it Georgian, it was, in fact, Victorian. I don't know and I can't say that I care. It was magic. Most of the houses in the row had been pulled down to make office blocks so Aunt Grace's house was outlined against an enormous sky. Girders propped it up. It was a very perilous-looking house surrounded by concrete and tarmacadam. Aunt Grace's house had the only garden, the only real garden, left in the row. All the other gardens were car parks, even when the original house remained. There was a mews house at the end of the garden and you went through the door and through the musty, damp-smelling mews into a kind of cinder space. Aunt Grace could never quite explain about the cinders.

"It's probably for drying," she said. "You know, feet get wet, earth gets wet, cinders are dry."

Aunt Grace was profoundly bored by architecture and explanations. Rather like Mum. If a thing was, it was. A homesick garden didn't need explanation. It just grew. And the homesick garden did grow. There were two slightly curving cinder paths edged with that red stuff that looked like twisted rope. "Or a long strangled red worm," said Aunt Grace. There was a garden chair on the little lawn near to the house. "The Clearing," Aunt Grace called it. She said you couldn't really call it a lawn because of the weeds and the muddy patches. It was simply an absence of undergrowth. There was a walkway over the back basement to the back door. Dad said—before or later—that it was an intact example of an Irish Urban Garden of the Previous Century—or something like that.

"Somewhat overgrown of course," said Dad.

Grace said that buddleias might be weeds but they attracted the butterflies. The garden was full of them that summer. She said she *preferred* lilacs spindly and long with weeds underneath them.

"Wild flowers *I* call them," said Aunt Grace.

"Oh," she said on that first seven-year-old morning as she stood on the walkway in the sun. "Oh, doesn't the garden look lovely!"

I was hungry because, on that first morning, I hadn't been able to eat the breakfast Mum had given me and I didn't much fancy the tired takeaway that Aunt Grace called breakfast and I was trying to get her to the shops and some kind of normality. Cereal, milk, bread, butter, I was thinking to myself. She'd taken away my panic on the canal but I was still uneasy. Her kind of joy was very close to chaos.

"We're not going to play in the garden, are we, Aunt Grace?" I asked. I knew she was an adult but she was a very childish sort of adult. Besides adults always thought that gardens were suitable places for children to play in. Who knew, Grace, demented-child-adult might trap me in this garden and make me play games. I looked at the bins under the walkway and Aunt Grace looked back at me over her shoulder.

"No, we're not going to play games. We're going to engage in a profound emotional discussion of an intellectual sort, accompanied at appropriate times by physical movement."

"I don't like movement, Aunt Grace," I said. "I like to stay still."

"Still and safe," said Aunt Grace. "Yes, well, I can see that. 'Here I am where I longed to be.'...Perhaps you'll be a nun when you grow up."

"I don't want to be a nun. I want *home*."

"Well," said Aunt Grace, "that's what it's all about. Homes and homesickness. If we sit down on this garden seat you can tell me three things that make you feel homesick and

I'll tell you three."

"Aunt Grace, that seat is wet."

"Does that make you feel homesick?"

"Everything makes me feel homesick," I said, sitting down on the damp slats in my new, crisp cotton dress. Mum had ironed it before she left. "*Everything*...No real food, no breakfast. You don't behave like family!" Aunt Grace put her arm around me and squeezed. It wasn't a very comforting squeeze, more a jerk.

"I'm not your family. I'm just Grace. You didn't ask for me and I didn't ask for you but here we are. I'm not really in charge of you. Do you see what I mean?" She said this very quickly, looking me in the face. I didn't see what she meant but I knew that she meant it.

"Yes, sort of."

"We're stuck," said Aunt Grace. "We're stuck with each other and we'll just have to make the best of it."

"Does that mean you don't want me?" I asked.

"Do you want *me*?" asked Aunt Grace. "The point is we don't know each other. We don't know if we want each other."

She closed her eyes and lay back against the sun.

"I feel homesick for my father who made me feel safe. I feel homesick for the right sort of mother I never had and for a coal fire."

I didn't want to know about fathers and mothers just then but the coal fire interested me.

"Why a coal fire?"

"Because my father loved coal fires and my mother always said it was too much trouble. We had ugly gas fires instead. That's three things. What about you?"

"The bamboo handle on the lavatory chain which Dad

put on. It was the handle of an umbrella and it bumps against the lavatory wall. It annoys Mum but it makes her laugh. At least it used to make her laugh. The smell of the real coffee that Dad makes when he gets up..." I looked at Aunt Grace but she was still lying back with her eyes half closed. The buddleias moved their long branches in the sun.

"The sound of Dad's key in the lock when he comes home at night and I know it's safe."

Aunt Grace opened her eyes and looked at me.

"Well, that's pretty good," she said. "But what about Mum? Don't you miss her at all? I'll race you to the end of the garden. You take this path and I'll take that one."

As I squeaked painfully and puffily along the cinder path I thought it was unfair. I did love Mum. I did, I did. But Mum had gone away. She'd left me.

By the time I got to the end of the cinder path—well ahead of Aunt Grace in the race—I knew something else. Dad had left me too.

"Too busy. Men are always too busy, that's the first rule."

I was thinking about that eight years later as I cycled towards Aunt Grace's flat.

❧❧❧

CHAPTER FOUR

Aunt Grace was lying in bed when I found her. Her room was in a mess. Drifts of newspaper all over the floor and half empty foil takeaway containers on the dressing table. There was a plastic pink bucket by the bed and the room smelled sweet and sick. The shutters were closed and every light was on. A powerful anglepoise lamp was aimed at Aunt Grace's sleeping face. She lay on her side in a still, wary, helpless position, curled up tight to keep away the sickness. Her radio was on, crackling and jabbering. Aunt Grace was whiffling noisily in her sleep, half-snore, half-whine. She looked dreadful but not alarming. Her face was swollen and pink in sleep but her hair, as far as I could see, was shiny and clean. I didn't know whether to wake her or not. It seemed enough just to have found her and I knew, from bitter experience, that the best thing, the only thing, to stop you feeling sick is to sleep. So I sat down on the wicker chair by the bed with the keys of the flat in my hand.

I'd come through the back way, into the mews and up the homesick garden and over the walkway. The back door of the house was locked—it never used to be—but I had the key for that too. Aunt Grace had given me the keys when I was twelve and Mum had locked me out of our house by accident. As a matter of fact Mum was always locking people out of the house—herself included. She was meant to leave the keys in a secret hiding place if she was going to be out when I came back but she was always changing the secret hiding place, "for security reasons," she said. This was nonsense, Dad said. It would be much safer to give me keys but Mum had this thing about "latch-key" children because she'd read an article about them. She seemed to think that giving me a key would be the first step on the road to drug-addiction and worse. Anyway, Mum was out and I couldn't find the key in any of her secret hiding-places so after I'd dug up half the front garden looking for keys I'd cycled over to Grace's and she found me waiting by her front door in the rain.

"You need keys," she said, as if I didn't know. "Everyone needs keys. Get Liz to give you keys to the house and I'll give you keys to this flat. But one thing," she said very seriously, "Come in the back way and don't tell anyone about it. I need some privacy."

Aunt Grace used the front door for privacy. She had one of those modern security arrangements. When someone rang the bell, she pressed a button and she could see the undesirable on a screen. She was never very pleased to see any unexpected visitor. She hated the phone too.

"It's always the last person you want to hear. The-longed-for-one never phones."

I'd suggested an answering machine but Grace said, "Think of Grandma," and we'd both shuddered. Grandma on record. It didn't bear thinking about. But the video arrangement pleased Grace enormously. She said it was ridiculous to have such a thing in a shabby flat that didn't have enough water—never mind a washing-machine.

"It does give me a sense of power, though," she said. "I can look and they can't see me and I can reject them without them ever knowing about it."

It was always difficult to tell whether Aunt Grace was in or out because, in the winter evenings, she always kept the shutters closed and her heavy curtains drawn. She was passionate about privacy. She said that after a day in school all her nerve-ends were exposed and waving in the breeze.

"Good teachers are always considerate, if not polite," she said. "In the evening I like to be rude all by myself." I didn't count, she said. She never felt the need to be rude to me. Partly because she knew if she *was* rude to me I wouldn't be offended or hurt.

It was true. I hadn't been offended or hurt when Aunt Grace disappeared. Grandma had been offended and even Mum had begun to curse when Grace didn't answer her phone. But it hadn't bothered me because I knew Aunt Grace wasn't doing it to *me*. She was doing it for herself.

Aunt Grace opened her eyes.

"Antonia, how did you get in?"

"Keys," I said, jangling them.

"Did you knock?"

"You know I always knock just in case you might be in bed with a famous married politician. I knocked and I said, 'It's Antonia,' and then I came in and there you were in bed whiffling like a porpoise in labour."

"Do porpoises whiffle in labour? Do porpoises go into labour? Surely not. It's odd the things teachers don't know because no one ever asks about them." Aunt Grace shut her eyes. "Does Elizabeth know you're here?"

"Mum doesn't know. Grandma doesn't know. Brian doesn't know. Dad doesn't know. I didn't know you were here until half an hour ago. I won't tell them either if you don't want me to. This place is in a mess, Grace. Do you mind if I clear it up?"

"Be my guest. Do you mind if I go back to sleep? Will you stay till I wake up again?"

This jolted me. I always wanted people to stay with me when I was sick, to be there when I woke up, but it had never occurred to me that Grace, with her passion for privacy, might need a face in the night.

"I'll stay," I said feeling like the Lady with the Lamp, important, powerful, compassionate. "You go back to sleep."

I had the most marvellous time. Mum sometimes says that I'm a lazy slut but there's no point in tidying and cleaning a tidy clean house. I mean there's no satisfaction in it. Baths are always better when you're dirty and you can watch the muddy water going down the drain afterwards. I never saw the point in a clean bath and I never could get worked up about polishing something that was shiny already. This attitude used to drive Mum demented.

"Of course it's clean *now*!" she'd say in our pre-Mini-Maid days when she was always trying to harness my precious talents to drudgery. "It's clean now but it won't stay clean unless you clean it!"

"It might, you know," I'd say. "Why don't you wait and see?"

Anyway, Aunt Grace's flat wasn't like that. Aunt Grace's flat was a challenge. It was so messy that it was quite easy to make it look better. I found a big black plastic sack in the Aladdin laundry basket where Aunt Grace used to hide treats and Christmas presents for me. The basket was full of sweaty, smelly clothes and the plastic bag was at the bottom but I unearthed it and threw most of the surface rubbish, crumpled tissues, newspapers, tinfoil containers into it. There was nothing to be done about the smell. I couldn't open the shutters in case it woke Grace, so I couldn't open the windows. I couldn't find air freshener or furniture polish or even perfume. But I got a saucepan—Aunt Grace had the only bucket—and filled it with hot water and washed down all the painted surfaces. Luckily Aunt Grace likes painted furniture better than the polished sort. She says her taste lies somewhere between chintz and kitsch so I did quite well with hot water and a damp tea-towel.

Cleaning is better than any other exercise. It's sort of moral. There, you say to yourself, there you filthy dressing-table. I've washed you and made you better. See that you stay that way.

The kitchen transformed me from Florence Nightingale into Pioneering Woman. Everything was greasy. The floor, the gas cooker, the walls, even, when I opened it, the fridge. How does grease get into a fridge? There was, naturally enough, no washing-up liquid. There was washing-powder but even I know that washing-powder stays around after the grease has gone. Tricky stuff, washing-powder. I decided that hot, hot water would be best. The hot tap was running cold by then and I didn't know where the immersion was. Like Aunt Grace and the porpoises. You never know the things you don't get asked. Still, Pioneering Woman boiled kettles and, six or seven kettles later, the kitchen was cleaner. A bit smeary because grease is hard to shift, but it did look respectable. And the fridge was really clean. It was also empty.

No milk, no eggs, no butter. Oh, there was half a dried-up-looking lemon but nothing else. I couldn't find any food on the shelves either. No cereal, no tins, not even sardines. Aunt Grace was having a baby. The poor little sod needs vitamins, I though, vitamins and calcium and protein. Do you get enough vitamins and calcium from Chinese takeaways? I hadn't a clue. I rather thought not, but then Chinese babies survive and multiply and why should I suddenly start getting adult and difficult and everything I hate most. It had always seemed to me that people who try to look after other people use that as a way of disapproving of them. "I'm good. I'm telling you how to live your life because your way of life is so much worse than mine. What? It suits you? It shouldn't suit you. Your way of life is bound to make someone-or-other miserable sooner or later." I'd nearly slipped into that trap myself. Vitamins and grease, tidiness and calcium. All ways of disapproving of Aunt Grace. Mum has her sloppy moments but our house is shining clean even if the glasses are a bit smeary sometimes. Window-cleaners and Mini-Maids visit it regularly. Despite all Mum's worries, or perhaps because of them, it is what you'd call a well-managed house. But I've never been so happy, so big, so swelling with self-importance as I was in Aunt Grace's messy rooms.

"Antonia?" Grace's voice came from the bedroom. I rushed in.

"It's so nice, the tidiness. You *have* been busy."

"I cleaned the kitchen too," I said smirking with pleasure. "Shall I change your bed? It looks a bit...uncomfortable." It did too. The pillows were squashed and leaking feathers. The sheets were grey and crumpled—but then Aunt Grace's sheets always were grey because she couldn't be bothered to sort whites from coloureds before she went to the launderette.

"You think I should get up and have a bath with the tea leaves while you change the bed and then I'll sit up on my nice crisp pillows and have a nourishing hot drink?" said Aunt Grace. She'd seen through my fantasies.

"Sorry," I muttered, feeling silly. Why are fantasies so much more pleasant when no one else is around. I had had a marvellous time cleaning up.

"Oh Antonia," said Grace, "I like you being here but I DO NOT NEED HOT DRINKS. I'm spiky and tired and no one ever told me that pregnancy would be like PMT and nausea combined in one unlovely parcel."

"Aunt Grace," I said. I don't usually call her Aunt Grace to her face since she asked me not to. "Grace will do," she'd said. But I'd been rebuffed, told off and I didn't feel very kind. "Aunt Grace, Brian is looking for you and he's driving Mum half-mad. He turns up every evening. He walks in the door and opens the fridge as if he owned the place. He drinks all her beer. Aunt Grace, if you don't want Brian, couldn't you tell him that?"

Aunt Grace simply didn't answer.

"I think I'll go back to sleep now," she said looking like Grandma in one of her more self-pitying moments. Me the Martyr.

"Shall I stay?" I asked, which was very brave of me. Suddenly I wanted to get out of that flat with its blazing lights and its lonely suffocating smell. However bad home was, it was at least lively. And Mum might yell at me, in fact she often did, but the yelling never exposed my fantasies or made me foolish.

"No, you go home. Don't worry about me," said Grace. Of all the phrases in the English language that I hate most, "Don't worry about me" is top of the list. What it means is that yes, you *should* worry about me but there's nothing you can do *for* me. My tragedy is very great and you're incapable of dealing with it. Grandma was always asking people not to worry about her. "For I won't be here very much longer," she'd say with a sad little smile. Fat chance.

"I won't worry about you, Aunt Grace," I said. I wasn't going to stand this nonsense from Grace, strong Grace, independent, funny Grace.

"I won't worry about you but I'll call around tomorrow because *it's my duty.*" That'll fix her, I thought, that'll raise a spark. But no. Aunt Grace opened her eyes briefly and said, "Well come if you want," and then closed them again.

Perhaps, I thought as I cycled home, perhaps there was something in this business about vitamins and calcium. Or perhaps Aunt Grace was beginning to suffer from premature senile dementia, the result of too much monosodium glutamate in all those takeaways. Or perhaps, oh ghastly thought, it was all in the blood. Perhaps self-pity was hereditary and when all those baby-making hormones got active it just *came out.*

❦

Mum was quarrelling with a Christmas tree when I got home. I'd come in the door with my key and there was Mum, embracing a fat fir in the dining room. There were three wet plastic bags on the floor. One of them was tied up like a balloon with a knot at the top. Dad's Christmas tree-stand, all restrained celtic curlicues, was poised to receive the tree. But Mum was waltzing feebly around the bay window with the fir. It was trembling and rocking against it.

"This is the last time, the very last time," said Mum, "I do what he says."

"Mum," I said, "Mum, are you all right?"

Mum poked her face through the branches and spikes.

"I am *not* all right. I am imprisoned by a Christmas tree and your father says the plastic bag with the water has to go into that black thing with the curls so the tree won't shed but the bags keep on bursting and I can't even hold up the tree. It's too big, Antonia, it's too big. How's Grace?"

This was just like Mum. You could never fool her for more than two minutes.

"Grace?" I said as if I'd never heard of her.

"People keep on having to explain who Grace is these days. First Brian, now me." Mum grumbled as she tried to take her hair out of the spikes. "Grace, my sister, your aunt. You've just been to see her. You're looking after her, I suppose, but you'd better drag her out of there before I do it. Because I *will* do it. I'm fed up with Brian. Yes or no, she has to say something."

At this point Mum's unequal struggle with the tree came to an end. It toppled over and fell on the full plastic bag, which burst and spilled all over the brown carpet.

"I told your father that would happen," said Mum sounding satisfied. "I told him I couldn't manage plastic bags full of water *and* Christmas trees." She jumped over the tree and grabbed her cigarettes and lighter from the dining-room table.

"That's better," she said, lighting one. "When's Grace coming out of purdah? Why is she in purdah? Don't answer if you don't want to. I'm madly curious but I'm not in the business of persecuting people."

There's no point in asking Mum how she knows things. I doubt if she knows herself. I once asked her how she knew, when no one else knew, that a friend of hers had got married in secret. Mum shrieked with laughter. "I just looked at the third finger on her left hand. There was a wedding ring on it. I've got a terribly obvious mind." But it's more than that. I mean the ring was there but no one else saw it. Mum only has to step into a taxi and the driver will tell her all about his life as an alcoholic and how his wife left him two years ago. That actually happened. And that was only a short journey too, from Ranelagh to O'Connell Street. God knows what would happen if Mum took a taxi to Tallaght. It's not that she's wise. Her own life's a mess, after all. But she'll ask one question, one very simple question and the next thing a total stranger will spill out his life story. Perhaps she's a witch.

When I was a kid, Mum used to parade the school playground at break-time to prevent some of the other children from throwing milk bottles at the passing buses. The headteacher had got upset about this disturbing new fashion and—naturally—spilled the beans to Mum. So down came Mum in her big black hat every break-time. The milk-kids used to call her "The Witch" because she never said anything or did anything. She'd just follow the troublemakers around in her big black hat.

"You're a witch, Mum," I said as I helped her to right the tree. We propped it against the wall to think about after Mum had finished her next cigarette.

"No I'm not," said Mum. "I knew you'd seen Aunt Grace because you've got her keys on your belt. I know that keyring. You always did keep her keys separate."

"I wonder," said Mum later when we'd got the tree into plastic bag in celtic tree-stand. "I wonder if I should hire a private detective?"

I dropped the crib and Joseph, Mary and assorted angels and wise men fell on the two remaining damp plastic bags on the floor.

"Why, Mum?" Mad thoughts of divorce and Dad cavorting with a blonde on the hotel kitchen floor flashed through my mind.

"For Brian," said Mum. "There's something very odd about it all. Grace hiding. Brian not finding her but pretending he wants to. I mean if you could find her surely he could. And Grace, Grace is really odd. She was never very bad at saying no before. Always saying no," said Mum with the flex of the fairy tree-lights in her teeth, "always saying no when we were children."

"*Don't* Mum!" I yelled. "Don't bite the flex!"

"It's not connected," said Mum checking the socket. "No, I knew it wasn't." Sometimes I think she's quite mad.

"It is very odd, you know," Mum went on. "And I can't find out myself. I don't really have the range."

"What range?"

"I can't go to America or Australia. I mean I wouldn't know if he was lying if he said he'd come from somewhere he hasn't come from, if you see what I mean. I haven't asked him either. I usually just ask if I want to know something," said Mum biting off a bit of thread she'd used to secure a silver shell. "People tell me too. But Grace isn't there to ask and Brian would lie if I asked him anything. He tells a lot of lies," said Mum thoughtfully. "Silly lies. Get-found-out lies. He told me he'd left us beer in the fridge and he hadn't!"

Clearly this had been a blow. I could just see Mum dashing to the fridge hoping to find some new rare form of beer brought by Brian. Australian beer or American beer brought in that day by plane. And then nothing but the same old Amstel, only less of it.

"It wasn't the beer," said Mum with dignity. "It was the

silly lie. People who tell obvious get-found-out lies about small things are usually telling enormous whoppers about big things. And I think Grace is frightened of something she suspects about Brian. So instead of just asking him about it, she goes away and hides. And I think Brian wants this baby—or doesn't want to lose it—so he's afraid of finding Grace in case she might ask him the right sort of wrong question. That's what I think," said Mum.

Strange standing there with Mum and listening to her fantastic theories and feeling for the first time that day, well, safe. A wobbly Christmas tree in the window, great patches of damp on the floor. Mum biting flex without checking the socket first and God had returned to his Heaven. All was right with the world. Better anyway.

❧❧❧

CHAPTER FIVE

S omewhat better. It wasn't the best of times. It wasn't the worst of times. It was the strangest, most jumbled-up time I have ever experienced. Up to now I have been trying to remember that time in sequence. It should have been simple. I mean I know the dates. It only takes nine months to make a baby and so on. But remembering things in sequence seems false. Because I simply can't remember them that way. The odd thing is that I can clearly and absolutely remember things happening *on the wrong dates*. Mum says I was upset. Dad says it's very understandable. Sometimes I think that they're reinventing time. I've got it right. They've got it wrong. But I suspect they're right. I was, as Mum says, very upset at the time. I'd lost Grace. Oh, I went to her flat every day. I tidied, I brought food. I didn't say anything about Mum knowing or not knowing. Mostly I didn't say anything at all and she didn't either. She got out of bed. She got dressed. Gradually she turned out the lights and opened the shutters. She was painfully polite and utterly absent. She thanked me automatically as if she had no idea what she was thanking me for.

Mum watched my comings and goings. I could see her biting away the pent-up questions. She'd start to ask me something and then she'd tell me something instead. She'd gone to the private detective. Not at all sleazy, she said, and sounded disappointed. "Probably not very efficient either," she said. She'd just got paid masses of back-money by her awful advertising agency, which wouldn't cover the cost but it was a bonus, wasn't it? She wasn't motherly. Mum rarely is motherly, but she never went out any more before I came home. She was always there, waiting.

Late one night on my way to the shower—I had endless soothing showers at that time—I heard Dad saying to Mum, "What's wrong with Antonia? Is she anorexic or something? She isn't eating. She isn't smiling. She's working like a little devil and she seems to have lost her sense of humour."

I must say I eavesdropped at that point. It's not hard to hear Mum and Dad at night because they always talk at the top of their very clear voices. I suppose they've been quarrelling for so long that they've learnt to pitch their voices at strife level. Eavesdropping just means staying in the hall.

"Antonia's upset about Grace," said Mum.

"*I'm* upset about Grace," said Dad angrily. "I don't starve and lose my sense of humour."

"Yes, well," said Mum, "You were never noted for your sense of humour anyway. Grace said something to Antonia and it hurt. Grace was more than a mother for Antonia. She was companion, friend, heroine, all in one and now Grace is hurt and Antonia is finding that hurt people aren't nice people. She's also finding that no one person is perfect, that friendship, that kind of friendship is a bit of a lie and that most people who love each other hate each other from time to time."

"Aren't you pleased?" said Dad who always leaves a bit of a barb in his tail.

"No," said Mum. "I thought I would be though. Antonia will never hero-worship me. Well, girls don't hero-worship their mothers. But it seems a pity that she has to lose someone to hero-worship, too soon. It's a great feeling, loving someone like that. It's a terrible feeling suddenly realising that you're all on your own. You know that no-one will ever love you the way you love you."

"I love *you*," said Dad.

"Well," said Mum briskly, "You couldn't possibly love me the way I love me."

Mum had obviously told Dad that I knew where Grace was. I would have thought that betrayal at one time, when I still had Grace, but now I thought that Mum couldn't have been nicer if she'd known I was eavesdropping. Did she know? Was that a prepared speech? I was sick of thoughts like that. I felt safe now at home but how long would that last? Would Mum change? Would Dad? They were both being so nice to each other—and to me—that it seemed only too likely. They weren't quite real at the moment so this safety was something that could shift under my feet. I just wished that they would quarrel again so I'd know where I was.

On Christmas Eve the sky fell in. Mum was in the kitchen cooking. On Christmas Eve Mum boils the spiced beef. She rolls out the Jus-Rol puffed pastry and makes mince pies.

"Homemade, how are you," she snarls. "I make better pastry than his mother ever did because I use Jus-Rol. They could try that in an ad. They could also tell you that it's slavishness that counts at Christmas. It's not the pastry. It's the pain. I hate pastry and flour and rolling-pins but they haven't invented a mince pie that can be homemade without them. Yuch!" And Mum, being Mum, sprays flour all over the kitchen floor. On the other hand Mum tunes in to the Christmas carols on the radio. I've seen her cry into the flour when the solo boy soprano starts with "Once in Royal

David's City." Mum sings along in her thready little voice, worn out with too much smoking.

Anyway this Christmas Eve, Mum was baking and boiling and crying and having, as far as I could tell, a perfectly splendid time, when the bell rang.

"Antonia!" roared Mum.

I was up watching television. There isn't room for anybody else in the kitchen when Mum starts on her Christmas Eve stint. And Mum won't have television in the kitchen. She says that the radio leaves her hands free but I think she wants would-be TV watchers out of her way. She does a lot of dreaming, does Mum with her radio. You can just see her making pictures in her head. But she doesn't like being interrupted so she's installed this ship's bell in the hall which she clangs if anyone has the nerve to ring the front doorbell. *I'm* supposed to answer the front door when I hear the ship's bell. It clanged. I opened the front door. There was this little blonde woman standing on the step. She was crying. She was thin, very thin and wearing a fur coat. A fur coat! Think of all the poor animals. Actually I rarely do. I mean I eat meat and walk on leather, for heaven's sake. But there was something terrible and pathetic about this little lady standing in our porch wearing fur when that's simply not done anymore and obviously she didn't know it. And her tears were making white tracks down her poor, thin, over-made-up face.

"Come in," I said.

"I don't want to bother you. It's a bad time to come, Christmas Eve. Is your Mum in?"

She wasn't Dad's blonde. That was clear. She was blonde all right but her voice was Australian, and not confident Australian like you hear on *Neighbours*. It had a whining cringe to it. Dad likes women who stand up to him. Also he's a snob. He'd never go for an over-made-up peroxide blonde with the wrong sort of accent. This woman looked like someone Mum would like because obviously she had problems. Mum isn't ever snobbish about problems or about anything else.

"Mum's in," I said. "She's crying in the kitchen." I dragged the woman in. "Mum's crying because it's Christmas and she always gets het up about Mary and the manger." I was gabbing and rushing because, suddenly, I knew who this woman must be. This was Brian's wife. As Mum would say, who else could it be?

"Mum," I said as I opened the kitchen door, "Mum, this is a woman who wants to see you."

Mum was red-eyed and flour-spattered. "Oh," she said.

"I said to your daughter I didn't want to bother you," said the woman in a quick, fussy voice. "I know it's Christmas and I'm sorta desperate. I came to spend Christmas here with my husband and he isn't *here*!"

And then she sat down at the kitchen table and started sobbing as if her heart would break.

"Oh dear, oh dear," said Mum rushing across and patting the woman's fur shoulders with her floury hands. "Oh dear. Husbands rarely are where they're supposed to be, particularly on Christmas Eve," she said with a baleful look at the clock. Dad had been working lunch at the hotel this Christmas Eve. He should have been back hours, well one hour, ago.

"Who is your husband?" asked Mum. "And why should he be here?"

"Not here in this house," said the woman, sounding irritated. "Here in *Dublin*. I went to his hotel. He wasn't there. He said he would be there but he wasn't. He told me about your family in his letters. He said you'd been 'A home from home.' He doesn't like home so I suppose there's a woman about. He thought the home business would make me feel better. It didn't, you know. The more lies he tells the more details he gives. The details are always OK. He has no imagination," she said as if that made it worse. "But the story is always wrong. The story is never true."

"Did you come from Australia?" I asked. "All that way?"

"No I did *not*! Did he tell you that? I did not. I'm a British citizen. I live in Birmingham. With him. Well I sometimes live with him. I did come from Australia. Brisbane as-a-matter-of-fact." She said it all in one gulp. "I wish I'd stayed there."

"Well you can always go back if you want to," said Mum calmly. I could see that she was thinking about kangaroos and flying doctors. She's always loved the thought of Australia. "All that space," she says dreamily as if she could see the tiny figures of Dad and me diminishing on a fading skyline.

"But you must tell me who you are?"

"You mean you don't know?" It seems snobbish to tell it the way she said it, "You mean yu don't naow?"

"No," said Mum. "I don't."

"You let a perfect stranger in out of the night to cry on your Christmas table and you don't know!" (I can't do the naow bit again.) "You don't know! Your daughter knows. All that talk of Australia. *She* knows."

"You're Brian's wife," I said. I felt witch-like, like Mum in her black hat. Is magic hereditary? But of course as Mum always says, it isn't magic. It's simply guess-work, based on fact. And I was fairly sure that Mum had known this was

Brian's wife as soon as she came through the door. Mum, for some reason, was stalling.

"I'm Brian's wife," said the woman, "I'm Marie. How do you do?" And she held out her hand to Mum, who grasped it in her own floury paw.

"Pleased to meet you," she said. Perhaps she did watch *Neighbours* in her spare moments.

"I'm Brian's wife," said Marie. "But what I want to know is where Brian is and what sort of story did he tell you?" At this point there was the sound of a mighty rushing wind, which meant someone had opened the front door. There was a crash (door slamming) and a stumble.

"I'm drunk!" carolled Dad from the hall. "I'm very very drunk. I've been drinking and drinking and drinking since lunch time and now I'd like to pinch a fat lady's bottom. Where is my wife, my moderately fat wife? Not that her bottom is fat. It's just her middle."

"Do you have to put up with that all the time?" said Marie, sounding awed.

"Not often," said Mum who'd got the giggles. "Not half often enough. I'm the one who drinks around here. He only gets festive once every decade. I think he must have taken to the Leeson Street strip and got involved with too many Tequila Sunrises. He's a very innocent drinker. He thinks sweet is safe. Don't mind him. He's quite harmless."

"Oh-my-God!" said Marie.

❦

It was six o'clock on Christmas morning. There was a truly horrid sound from upstairs. Dad was being sick. Mum had left him a bucket so it was none of my business anyway. I flipped up the blind and looked out. It was still and quiet and peaceful. Just a few lights on in the road. Perhaps there were children rustling around under Christmas trees. I felt suddenly homesick for the way it had been. Stockings and stars and excitement in the morning. Aunt Grace coming at eleven, with, always, the most magic present of all. I wandered into the dining-room to look at the tree. This was my time in the house. The time when I owned it. There, under the tree, was the most enormous big box, a big crude cardboard box covered with ivy, the blackened sort which grew on the wall outside the dining-room. The ivy had been sprayed silver over the black and there was this notice on the front: FOR ANTONIA FROM SANTA. It's not when people are nasty to you that you want to cry. It's often when they're suddenly, unexpectedly, nice.

Santa had left a lot of presents for Antonia. Sweets and oranges, books, the best sort. Mum is very good at books. No scarves, which I hate, but two of those games which bubble and tumble in plastic before your eyes. From Dad, I guessed. And two tapes. Not Strauss waltzes or Beethoven, the only kind of classical music Mum can stand. Early Christian music, breathing prayer, the kind that Dad likes and I like which is odd since we're both much less naturally religious than Mum is. I mean none of us believes in God but Mum still lights candles in darkened churches and thinks it will work. "You weren't even reared a Catholic," says Dad, who was. "That's why," says Mum. At the bottom of the box there was this other little box. A black, velvet, rectangular box. On the top of the box there was a kind of cat's cradle of sticky-tape, grimy sticky tape, enclosing a white envelope. Fairly white. Mum never could manage parcels. Inside was a card:

Dear Antonia,

When I was fifteen my godmother gave me these pearls. I'm handing them on to you because I love you. I know, I know you'd hate me to mention it but I do anyway.

Much love, Elizabeth...Your Mother.

❦

I was kneeling, gloating over these treasures when Marie came in. She'd stayed the night.

"We can't send her away," Mum had said. "It would be far too much like no room at the inn."

Actually I thought Marie would have stayed even if we'd tried to throw her out. Marie was the staying sort.

The dining-room was cold. We don't have central heating. We just turn on gas fires—there's one in almost every room—when we want to stay in a room. Most of the time we stay colder than other people. The hall is nearly always frigid.

The spare room is worse than frigid.

"Hey!" said Maria. "Is this Santa's stocking? Look at the box with the silver ivy on it. That's beautiful. You *know*.

I did know.

"It's funny," said Marie. "How you miss the things you never had. My Mum, Maw we called her, died when I was little. Dad was a good sort of bloke. There was always a present for every one of us at Christmas—but never anything like this. Maybe it's the climate," she said, shivering in Mum's old summer dressing-gown. "Christmas isn't the same at home. When it's that hot you don't really get to believe in Santa and sleigh-bells. Never missed it really until Birmingham. After I got married in Birmingham I got to understand about Santa. I couldn't wait to have a baby and a Christmas tree." Marie had taken off the make-up and tied up her hair. She looked now like an elderly, tired child. "We got the Christmas tree. It's green plastic and I take it out every year. The baby never came. Your Mum's lucky."

"Yes," I said. I could feel the pressure building in Marie's fiddling. She was tidying up wrappings, picking tinsel off the carpet...quick, nervous, waiting. She was going to ask a question and I was going to have to answer it.

"Who's Brian's woman, Antonia? Like I said to your Mum, he never did go in for family life. So if he's seeing your family there has to be a woman there, somewhere. It's not your Mum. I wouldn't ask if I thought that. Your Mum isn't that sort of a lady."

"What sort?" I asked, feeling vaguely insulted on Mum's behalf.

"Your Mum's straight," said Marie. "Brian likes something more complicated. If he'd wanted straight he would have stuck to me. Brian likes what he can't have. Not someone who would say that. But someone who wouldn't."

"It sounds complicated," I said.

"No it isn't," insisted Marie. "It's kind of obvious once you know how. He wants to make someone reject him and then he can blame his failure on them. He's one of nature's willing victims." And she grinned. "So who's the lady in the case? It's not going to hurt *that much*. It's not the first time. But I need to know."

The trouble was that I knew that it was going to hurt much more than *that much*. A lady, straight or complicated, is one thing. A baby is another.

But this was Christmas day and Grandma was going to be here, as sure as God made little apples (did he?) at four o'clock. Someone was going to have to answer Marie's question, sooner or later. It might as well be me.

"It's my Aunt Grace," I said in a gabble. "She's having a baby. We all think it's his baby. But she won't see him and she doesn't seem to want to marry him or anything like that. Mum would kill me if she knew I'd told you this, but someone had to, didn't they?"

"Someone did have to," said Marie slowly.

❦❦❦

CHAPTER SIX

D ad said it was all my fault. From the way he said it you'd think that Marie had split her wrists open in the bath or gone down to the canal to drown like a dog. In fact Marie stayed pretty calm. She just kept saying "I want that baby!" over and over again. Mum didn't say it was my fault. Mum is keener on small sins like not doing the washing up, than she is on big ones. She says she feels too guilty to contemplate any moral failure that isn't strictly measurable. "In other people, that is," she once said. "I was born with the certain knowledge of my own sin so I find it difficult to think about other people's. I'm sure I'm much guiltier than anyone else can possibly be." But Dad doesn't seem to suffer from guilt. Not that sort of guilt anyway. I think he thinks that life is pretty simple. That's the Catholic in him. Mum behaves as if there are very few sins—except her own— just constant muddle. But Dad has a tidy mind. He thinks he can track down a sinner—not that he'd call anyone that—and make sense of the muddle.

"Why did you tell Marie about Grace, Antonia?" Dad kept on saying. "Did you have to do that? Did you want to hurt Grace? To pay her back. Did she hurt you that badly?"

"Oh for God's sake!" said Mum.

"I just told Marie the truth!" I roared. I hate Dad when he tries to get psychological. I don't like people trying to wander about in my mind. "Did you want to have Christmas dinner with Grandma wondering who this was and Marie being humiliated when Grandma found out? 'Oh but Brian can't be married, dear, my daughter Grace is having his baby.' I can just hear her, can't you? You're a big ass! Marie was going to find out anyway. How long did you want her to wait? Until you could be polite about it? She asked me a direct question and I gave her a direct answer and I don't know why you have to make such a big deal about it. I can't understand why you want me to feel wrong about it. It was honourable to tell her. Perhaps you can't imagine that," I said sarcastically. "A sense of honour?" I was being a bit histrionic, I knew, but it felt good. "You don't lie to guests in your house, I just told her the truth, that's all."

"I have to think that this was manipulative," said Dad, unmoved by my passion.

"Oh my God," said Mum again.

If anyone was manipulative, Marie was. She'd declared herself, now she hung around. When I say that she was manipulative, I don't mean to say that I didn't like her. I did. But she had the sort of staying presence that weak people often have. She occupied our spare room, possibly the coldest room on earth. The spare room has no heater or gas fire and it has, as far as I can see, no ventilation either. When Mum sleeps in there the room reeks of cigarette smoke in the morning and she has to open the window wide to air the place. Mum explained all this to Marie. She could stay, but...but the room was cold and it wasn't ventilated so you should really, said Mum, sleep with the window open. No you couldn't use an electric fire because of our ancient wiring and the fact that the only socket in the room was a light socket.

"Not," said Mum, "a power-point."

We have a big house. It should have four big bedrooms.

But Mum turned one of them into a sitting-room and the other into her study. So there's only one cold, mouldy, smelly spare room.

"People can come to stay," says Mum, "but they don't stay long." Marie showed every sign of being the exception to this rule.

On Christmas Day, after what Dad called my "Unnecessary and Untimely Revelations," Marie tactfully disappeared around one o'clock and avoided both Grandma and Christmas dinner. This turned out to be a smart move. Christmas dinner was pretty horrible. Mum was distracted, Grandma was angry in a suspicious sort of way and Dad, well Dad was plain sick. When he cut into the turkey he discovered that the inside was mostly raw because Mum had spent the morning dealing with my Unnecessary and Untimely etc. and listening to Marie wittering on about how she wanted this baby and trying not to answer her questions about Grace. What did Grace look like and where did she live were the main ones. Marie kept on asking if Grace had a better figure than she, Marie, did. I thought this was ridiculous because Marie didn't have what you could call a figure at all. She was just straight up and down and not very much of that, as Grandma would say. But Mum said vaguely that she'd never really thought about Grace having a figure because she was always so preoccupied with her own and now that she came to think of it, the last time she'd noticed that Grace had any shape at all was in 1976 when they both went swimming at Seapoint. "It was quite sunny that day," said Mum helpfully, "and Grace was thinner than I was, taller too, of course, but then she always is. That was the day I realised that I'd have to give up wearing a bikini. It was just after Antonia, of course. I'd got a bit flabby, no stretch marks though," said Mum with pride. "Since then Grace took to the layered look. She's tall, I do know that. She's not fat, I think, but all those clothes make her look bulky."

As for Grace's address, since Mum didn't know where Grace was definitely or for certain, she wasn't prepared to give Marie an address. "It's difficult, you see," said Mum looking earnest. "She's an unmarried mother—well, will be—and a teacher. I can't have people making enquiries at her flat."

All of this was complete gobbledegook but it was so mad and pseudo-logical and wrapped up in meaningless innuendo that Marie gave up and said that she'd go to the hotel and collect her luggage and see if Brian had turned up or left a message and please, could she stay another night with us if he hadn't done either of those things?

"I feel at home here," she said pleadingly.

There is nothing stronger than people who can admit to being weak.

"You and Brian both," said Mum a trifle bitterly, thinking, no doubt, of the beer. And then she went into this unwelcoming routine about the spare room, which didn't seem to deter Marie one bit.

So, after Marie had gone, Mum put the turkey in the oven and forgot to turn on the gas, which meant, of course, that when Dad cut into the golden skin he found raw flesh underneath.

"Some of it must be cooked." said Mum. "I remembered I forgot at least two hours ago."

"There *is* a layer of cooked flesh," admitted Dad. "But the rest...

"Well let's eat the cooked part and ignore the rest," said

Mum snappily. I could see she was getting angry. After all she'd had to deal with my Unnecessary etc., and Marie too, while Dad was still sleeping.

"Oh EEElizabeth," said Grandma, "forgive me. I can't eat raw flesh or even cooked meat that's been in contact with raw meat. I read something about it in *The Irish Times* the other day. Salmonella or some such thing. The fact is that raw and cooked don't mix."

Grandma was wearing a pink paper hat. We'd had the crackers while Mum was crashing around the kitchen trying to convince herself that the turkey was cooked. The trimmings were wonderful. They usually are. Sprouts and chestnut stuffing and mushroom gravy. Mum is very good at trimmings. She's just not very good at meat.

"It's so boring," she says. "If you watch it it doesn't get cooked and if you don't watch it, it gets burnt."

Maybe Mum hadn't been stonewalling with Marie. Maybe she is mad and illogical and full of meaningless innuendo.

"Anyway," said Mum, "It's mixing *cold* raw and cooked meats in supermarkets and delicatessens that's the problem. And they have to be different kinds of meats too. How could a turkey argue with itself?"

Dad put down the carving-knife.

"I'm very sorry, everyone, I don't feel well," he said and charged out the door. Mum persuaded Grandma to have trimmings and Grandma volunteered to "try a little skin, dear, just so as not to hurt your feelings."

Gradnma stirred the food around the plate with a fork. She didn't eat much but then she never does. The end of the meal was a relief.

"Well," said Mum as I took away the plates, "let's get

drunk. Have some port everyone?" Dad had been given a very good port, a vintage year, he said, by a grateful wine-merchant. Question: Why was this wine-merchant grateful? Was Dad cheating in his buying? Impossible. First of all Dad wouldn't and second of all how could he? He was a cook and not a wine-waiter. But I knew that Dad valued that port. He'd been looking forward to drinking it slowly and carefully with Stilton, perhaps, and water biscuits, after an elegant dinner for two. Mum poured it out like lemonade.

I don't drink, never will and won't smoke either, ever. Half the girls in my class have a severe—I really mean that—smoking problem. They smoke the sort of cigarettes that even Mum says makes her experienced throat feel raspy. And they buy at least twenty a day. It's not allowed in school of course, so they all do it in the toilets. Every time I go into the toilets at school there's this terrible stink. One cubicle is locked and clouds of smoke drift over the top of the partition. And then there are giggles and coughs. It's not so funny. Mum says she took up smoking, deliberately, when she was seventeen. Can you imagine that?

"I was trying to slim," she said. But though smoking was supposed to be bad for you "in a vague sort of way" there was no very obvious hint then that it led to lung cancer and heart disease. That doesn't help Mum, who can't give it up now. When she heard about the smoking at school she could hardly believe it. "Do you mean they take it up knowing just how bad it is for them?"

I said that I didn't think they did know. They'd heard all the evidence of course but most of their parents smoke. Mum winced at this. And the parents are still alive, I told her. Since parents seem, well, old to most fifteen-year-olds, and since the parents in our school are ambitious people, high achievers, well then smoking can't be bad for you.

I can't understand why I said all that to Mum, who already feels quite guilty enough, when I didn't say it to Dad. Dad smokes too, less than Mum, but he doesn't show the slightest sign of guilt about it. So why attack poor Mum? Do guilty people attract blame just like weak people attract support?

Anyway I don't and won't smoke and I hope I'll never drink either. But I must admit that when Mum poured out Dad's precious port Grandma got a lot more amiable.

"That's very nice, EEElizabeth," she said, "very nice indeed. Some sort of cordial, I think. Very nice. Grace, Grace," Grandma adjusted her pink paper hat, "difficult for you about Grace. She once tried to kill you in your pram. Did you know that? Hit you with a sharp toy. There were sharp toys then," said Grandma, as if that excused it somehow. "In fact almost all toys were sharp. Grace took up a toy soldier, one of a whole set given to us by your father's brother who thought that this second baby would have to be a boy. I thought that too," said Grandma trying to look wistful. "In those days women went on having babies until they had a boy. Two was too much for me. I stopped trying. Anyway, Grace didn't like you from the start. She pretended to, of course. She was always a very *sly* child. She'd hug you so tight that you squealed. Robert said," (Robert was Grandpa) "Robert said that he'd seen her pinch you. I didn't want to believe that—then."

"It's all right, Mum," said Mum. "It's all right now. It's over. We're both grown up."

"It's not all right," said Grandma taking a great gulp of her port. "It would have been all right if we'd had a boy. Do you know how hard it is to have a baby, EEElizabeth? How hard, how thankless, how lonely, how painful?"

The gas fire purred. There were sounds of retching from upstairs. Poor Dad. The old rose-coloured curtains stirred slightly in a cold breeze. (Dad hadn't got around to double-glazing the dining room yet). It was a bad little scene, the sort that makes you think about death and fear. About being old and having nothing to look forward to. It was all leftovers. I was suddenly terrified. I wanted to get up out of my chair and run and scream and hear loud music and not stay here and listen to Grandma's terrible old voice. But I couldn't leave Mum.

"I do know about having a baby," said Mum. Her voice was high and angry. "I had a baby, remember. You hoped it would be a boy. And yes, it was some of the things you said it was. It was lonely and painful and hard—but not thankless. I didn't expect to be thanked. Having babies is selfish. You don't get neat little rewards for it. You don't get a boy just because that's what you thought you wanted. You get what you're given and if you can't accept that then maybe you don't deserve a baby at all."

"Well, you always were very sentimental, EEElizabeth," said Grandma downing her port and taking off her tired paper hat. "But look at Antonia here. She's beginning to look like a young spinster. Only Child." Grandma said it as if it was a dreaded disease. "Only Child. No friends that I can see. Totally absorbed in her own family. Too fond of Grace. Is that healthy?"

"The mean old *maggot!*" said Mum an hour later as we stood at the open front door waving goodbye and good riddance to Grandma's taxi. Mum was looking a bit tired and emotional. Her eyes were glittery and dangerous-looking. "The mean old maggot. I can't think how she always manages to make everything seem dirty—but she does. It's not true what she said, Antonia, you musn't think that. You don't look at all like a spinster. Nothing, of course, wrong with being a spinster even if you did look like one, which you don't. I mean, Oh God what do I mean?" Mum shut the front door and stood with her back against it. "I don't know what I mean. Tell me, do you mind about being an only child?"

I said I didn't. Quite liked it in fact. But I couldn't feel as indignant as Mum did about what Grandma had said. I think Mum was so terrified of the tiny nugget of truth in it that she felt she had to denounce it all as rubbish. It wasn't all rubbish. Some of it was rubbish but some of it was not. I don't think I look like a young spinster but the truth is that I don't really know what I do look like. I'm tall and skinny. Mum said this is most unfair since I eat chocolate and piles of cereal and she is so careful. Mum, naturally, doesn't count the calories in beer. I have thick brown hair. I have features in all the right places. I never get spots. My teeth are straight so I never needed a brace. But, and it's a big but, I seem to lack some mysterious quality that other, much more faulty, girls have. Boys don't get excited or interested when I'm about. Girls don't get jealous. Whenever anyone notices that I'm not a bad shape, they seem to be surprised about it.

"Why Antonia, you *do* have a good figure," they'll say when I wear my one-piece (no bikinis for me) to the school swimming-pool. "You know you're really quite pretty." Gosh. Goodness. Should I be grateful?

I'm not grateful because, you see, it doesn't work. People—well other girls—have been surprised on various occasions by the superior quality of my skin, my legs, my teeth, my hair. It's as if God had made me up in separate sections but had somehow forgotten to put the lot together and add a bit of oomph. What is oomph? Well sex-appeal, perhaps. That's the obvious lack. But in my case it's more complicated than that. I feel sometimes as if I exist in separate sections. I look in the mirror and notice my hair, my teeth, my fierce eyebrows, my fine skin but I can't see my own face. And if you can't see your own face how on earth can you make anyone else see it? At my best I feel normally homesick—"I can't go out at night because I want to stay at home." At my worst, well at my worst I know that I can't go out at night with boys—or even with girls— because there's something missing.

And the very worst thing is that no one ever asks me. I'm not there for me, at school, and therefore I'm not there for them.

☜☜☜

CHAPTER SEVEN

On New Year's Day I thought about making my New Year's resolutions but I couldn't see much point in it since I made some last year and they didn't have the slightest effect. So I've decided that resolutions are backward-looking, more about how you want *not* to be than what you want to be. I told myself that that was negative and then thought how nice it would be if one could make resolutions for other people. Everyone in this house could do with a resolution or two.

Marie spent the day crying in her room—loudly—and Mum was in bed having flu and Dad was out preparing what he calls a three-star special—each course deadlier than the last, he said—for a dinner-dance at the hotel. I felt surrounded by little pools of loneliness but somehow powerful, the way you do when everyone else is flat and you're upright. I wandered into Mum's room and asked her if she thought her flu was real flu or just-a-cold-and-Marie, and Mum opened one bleary eye and said she thought it was a bit of both plus not being able to get much sleep because sometimes she snores and Dad doesn't like it so when she has to share a room with him she tries to stay awake and *not* snore and that makes her exhausted.

"It's much easier sleeping in the spare room. I know it smells and has no air but if you open the bottom of the window and leave up the blind then you can wake up and read without disturbing anyone at six o'clock in the morning. You can watch the sky and the seagulls in the wind." Honestly, from the way Mum talks you'd think she loved mornings. In fact as soon as the sun comes up with any conviction at all, she winces and goes to sleep. She told me once that she was frightened of the dark and the night, that she likes to stay awake until the sun comes up so that she can be sure that it *has* come up. "Like seeing a ship through a storm," she said. Captain Mum. She says that if she sleeps in the dark, she wakes up in the middle of the night and thinks she is dead. Very neurotic. But I know the feeling. I've had it once or twice when I was away from home. You wake up and it's dark and you don't know where you are or who you are and then you wonder if you're asleep or dreaming or dead. And then you get into a kind of panic and stagger out of bed and slap yourself to prove that you're alive.

Sometimes I think I can understand Mum pretty well because she puts things I've felt into words and then at other times, thinking about Mum and Dad, and even Grace, makes my mind start to zing and zang which is what I call that kind of wiry whirry noise that starts in my head when I'm trying to understand something that's just out of my reach. School work never has that effect. It's either out of my reach altogether or well within it. And when it's done it's done. People are never done, you can't really control them. I've often thought of telling Mum how she could change her life by giving up guilt and standing up to Grandma and not minding what Dad says but when it comes to it I find I can't get the words out. It's easier to think resolutions for other people than it is to say them. I mean if I told Mum her life needed changing she might get annoyed, or hurt, which would be worse. Being sorry for people is frustrating.

Very frustrating, as I found out when I tapped on Marie's door, which is opposite to Mum's door. I could hear Marie crying in there and since I'd offered to bring Mum any little treat she fancied (in her case ice-cold beer in one glass and two aspirin in water in another), I couldn't pass by the sound of sobbing coming from the opposite room without trying to do something.

Marie didn't say "Come in!" She came to the door as if she was hiding something in the room behind her. She was wearing a long black nightie, flimsy and almost transparent You could see her poor thin legs quite clearly through it. She was also wearing her dear old fur coat, hunched up about her neck. It was all askew as if she'd been sleeping and sobbing in it. She was shivering.

"I just came to ask if you'd like anything? I could make you a hot water bottle, I think there is one somewhere. It's two o'clock in the afternoon," I added because, as far as I knew, normal sane people didn't stay in bed in black nighties and fur coats at two o'clock in the afternoon. Even Mum was claiming to be sick.

"I don't want anything," said Marie, gazing at me as if she did want something.

"Anything, anything," I gabbled. "I can get you anything. Wine, beer, food, books?" There were no books in the spare room and whereas I could quite well imagine how somebody could stay in bed indefinitely, I simply couldn't understand how anyone could manage that without a book. "A nice book—take your mind off things?" I knew I sounded like a demented Nanny in a book but I couldn't help it. There was something so childish and helplessly old-fashioned about Marie that she made me think of nursery comforts, hot milk and cod-liver oil and perhaps a nice walk in the freezing air if she couldn't—or wouldn't—cheer up. No wonder Nannies were such bullies.

"I don't want anything," said Marie again. "But you can come in if you like."

I didn't like. I wanted to run.

"There's nowhere to sit," said Marie aggressively, ushering me in. "Except the bed."

I sat on the bed and Marie got into it, trembling and fussing with the sacred fur.

"I tried to go and see your aunt. About the baby. I really did want that baby, you know."

I didn't know. I knew she'd told me she wanted it but that was different. I shut up.

"Your Dad gave me your aunt's address," (The traitor!!!) "He said it was better to have things all out in the open. I could talk to your aunt about the baby but I musn't bully her. He said that when I met her I'd probably feel happier about the baby. He said that she'd make 'a marvellous mother' as if, as if I was concerned about the baby, you know. But I wasn't. I just wanted it. I wanted it for me, not for it. Do you see?"

I did see. It was nice of her to ask me but I saw immediately. I suddenly liked Marie. Most adults who felt as she did, who wanted a baby as a possession, would have denied that to the death. I mean most adults really are possessive about their children but they always try to pretend that a child is like an environmental issue, a cause, something for which you act in its own best interests. Adults tend to leave out the basic things, as if they're ashamed of them. Marie didn't want the baby the way a social worker would want it. She didn't want it for its own good. She just wanted it.

It came into my mind as I stared at her little pinched, fur-edged face that she might, in fact, be quite a good mother. She looked like a mouse in a duvet but there was something very powerful about her all the same.

"I *did* go to the address your Dad gave me. I rang the bell but there was no-one there. And then I thought—you know the way you think outside front doors—I thought, what could I say? I want your baby because my husband is its father and then she'd say, well, where is he? Why doesn't he ask for it himself? And I don't know where he is, Antonia. I don't even know what he's doing this time."

"How do you mean, 'this time'?" I asked.

"Nothing," said Marie, cringing back in the bed. "Nothing, I don't mean anything."

And that was that. End of promising conversation. I did find a hot water bottle for Marie and filled it and took it up to her hanging out of my teeth because I was bringing up the tray with Mum's little treats at the same time. I nearly lost my teeth but I couldn't get a word out of Marie, who pretended to be asleep. She wasn't very good at it. Most people sleep with their mouths open. But Marie pretended with her mouth crimped shut and her two bony hands clenched around the collar of her fur coat. Either she was awake or she had the baddest of bad dreams. Probably both.

She stayed on though. She spent hours suffering in the spare room in a very private yet public way. You couldn't put a foot on the stairs without being conscious of her misery. At least that's what Mum said. I thought that Marie was beginning to run out of money. At the beginning she'd bought herself takeaways. "I don't want to put anyone to any trouble," she said. But now she started to raid the fridge at night. I knew because I did that too. "Oh no," she'd say when Mum invited her to yet another turkey casserole. "No, I won't intrude. Don't worry about *me.*"

It was hard, as Mum pointed out when she rose out of her bed, not to worry about someone who sat in your spare room crying, particularly if they refused to eat turkey casserole and you, (she, that is, Mum) had been granted two turkeys this season. Mum was cross because Dad had brought home yet another raw turkey after the dinner-dance. He said it was a gift and a favour and Mum wondered why the top chef hadn't snaffled it if he was so keen.

"His wife isn't a very good cook," said Dad thoughtfully. "Come to think of it, he isn't either."

Mum sighed and looked pleased and went on adding mushrooms and broccoli and even salad—salad!—to the ongoing turkey casserole which seemed to get larger every time I lifted the lid off the pot. It's an odd thing about turkey. It always smells ripe, that is, nearly bad, as if it had met too many unwholesome things in the farmyard. Mum called the smell "gamey" but she went on adding things. "Waste not, want not," she kept saying until Dad asked what she had put in the casserole.

"Turkey. You remember, turkey," said Mum wearily. "And other things too because I'm so tired of turkey." I think she was too tired to be angry any more. Upstairs you could hear Marie moving backwards and forwards. Mum twitched every time she heard an apologetic footfall.

"Turkey," said Mum again. "It's horrible I know. It's shredding and going separate. I'm going to throw it out." And she got a plastic bag and poured the whole horrible mess into the bag.

"That's waste," said Dad with a smile.

"I *know* it's waste," said Mum. "But it would be waste

eating it."

Smile, smile. They sparkled at each other. Two young things getting a bit older. They looked ridiculous—and sweet. I felt like crying when I looked at them and I never feel like crying when they quarrel.

The next day was bitterly cold. I woke up to frost on the window-panes and the terrible *thud* of cold weather. I know it doesn't make a noise but it feels a noise, even before you get up. Marie knocked on Mum and Dad's door at about midday and said that she was going away for a couple of days. Dad and Mum hate to be summoned before they emerge from their room. Mum can just about stand it but Dad can't. They play this game if anyone rings the bell or phones the house.

"*You* answer it," says Mum.

"No, *you* answer it," says Dad

"I'm not dressed," says Mum.

"Well you'd better answer it because it's always for you," says Dad.

That's true. It always is for Mum, the phone and the bell and the people who want to talk. That's not Mum's fault, exactly, but I wonder sometimes if Dad resents it a bit. They're not sociable, either of them. Mum simply loathes telephone calls, or so she says, but she is a passionate letter-writer and gets about quite a bit in an unwilling sort of way. She hates the idea of going places but once she's been invited and safely on her way she has a good time. And then she sparkles. Mum does sparkle, and so she gets invited somewhere else. A fact she bitterly and insincerely regrets afterwards. Mum can't help enjoying herself whatever she does and Dad can't help not enjoying himself. The odd thing is that Mum would like to be a bit more like Dad. I mean she does try not to enjoy herself or have fun, she just can't help it, that's all. She gets tragic sometimes and depressed. When she quarrels with Dad she can wander around for days with laser-beam eyes just flashing fury. She never says sorry. Dad always does. But even when Mum is being most vivid and indignant and unhappy, she's never down the way Dad is. She's always hopeful. I don't think she even knows what it is to feel joyless. Sometimes when I see Dad crouched over the kitchen table late at night, reading the early morning paper and listening to the sad sounds of ancient Church music—he doesn't even believe in God—sometimes then I wonder why, well, why he finds joy so difficult.

If Dad finds joy difficult, he finds mornings impossible. There was a noise of skirmishing and strangled yawns when Marie tapped at the door and Mum unbolted it, which made me feel a bit creepy from my vantage point at the open bathroom door. I hate it when they bolt the bedroom door and I hate it when they *un*bolt it. It's all so quiet and embarrassing and private and I know that I should have come to terms with the idea that my parents have a sex life but quite frankly I'd rather they didn't. I'd like them to be fond of each other, of course, but bolted doors are a bit sinister. It's as if they didn't belong to me any more. Marie said her bit about going away and Mum muttered something back and shut the door and then shot the squeaky bolt again. Dad hasn't got around to oiling it. Then I heard this thump, thump, and there was Marie (in her fur) skidding two suitcases down the stairs. They were leather-looking plastic ones with little wheels and zips. I knew that I should go out and help her but I'd only brought my T-shirt and bikini pants up to the bathroom and anyway I suddenly felt that Marie's time was over.

There are moments like that. It's a bit like feeling the noise of cold weather, the thud. Sometimes you feel a thud when everything's about to change. Watching Marie sliding the suitcases down the staircase in that secret way gave me a bad feeling. I felt angry because she was using the bald smooth edges of the carpet to give her suitcases a good slide. Mum hates that stair-carpet. She says it was a cheat because the fitter never put a proper lining under the risers—whatever they are—and consequently the carpet has these bare bits at the edges of the stairs. It didn't seem right that Marie was using Mum's poor stair-carpet to slide her suitcases down but then Marie didn't seem sad or pitiable anymore. There she was escaping, the furtive enemy. My friend had gone.

She had gone too. The front door slammed and the house felt empty. Why is there always something so sad about people going away, even if you don't trust them? The house had changed shape. Last night Mum and Dad and I had been in the kitchen worrying about Marie in the spare-room and we'd all been together worrying. And now there was a bolted bedroom and me in the bathroom in my T-shirt and bikini pants. I knew the couple of days was nonsense. You don't take two suitcases for a couple of days.

Marie had left the spare room door open—and the window. Flurries of sleety rain were blowing in onto the patchwork quilt, the pride of Mum's heart that she started making the time she took up arts and crafts. There was nothing—simply nothing—of Marie's in the room. She'd polished the little trays on the dressing table where her Boot's No. 7 used to be. She'd even emptied the waste-paper basket. There was no note, though I looked for one.

I knew Marie wasn't coming back.

"I don't understand it," said Dad when he got up. "She wasn't unpleasant. She didn't feel like a crook or anything. Why didn't she say she wasn't coming back?"

Mum blushed.

"I cashed, well I cashed a couple of cheques for her. Nothing much. I'm *sorry*. But it was my money. Why do you always behave as if my money was your money?" Mum asked Dad as if blaming him for her faults would make it all better. "I don't think it's fair!"

"It's *our* money," said Dad. "Mine, yours. Yours, mine and you wouldn't go on like that if you didn't feel so guilty."

"I don't feel guilty," said Mum angrily. "I just feel used and stupid. Grace makes a mess and lands us with Brian. Then Brian makes a mess and lands us with Marie. And now they've all disappeared, except Grace, and she's no use to anybody at all because she simply won't talk to us. She won't even talk to Antonia, will she Antonia?"

"Well no," I said. "But then I haven't seen her since Marie came. It was all too complicated. I couldn't feel sorry for them both at once, you see. But Mum," a sudden thought occurred to me. "Mum, what about your private detective?"

"*What* private detective?" roared Dad.

It could have been disastrous. A repeat performance of my Unnecessary and Untimely Revelations on Christmas Day. But this time was different. This time even Dad was in need of a spot of revelation. Dad was worried about the cheques and asked Mum if she'd taken them to the bank yet but she hadn't of course and when she found them— in the cosmetic section of her handbag—there were only two, each for twenty pounds on an English bank. They were post-dated and apparently Mum hadn't understood about sterling and neither had Marie. Mum had given Marie punts for pounds so even if the cheques bounced it wasn't a lot of money.

"I knew not understanding about money would come in handy some time," said Mum.

"Yes dear," said Dad with a sigh.

The truth was, I suspect, that he felt a bit of a fool himself. We'd all been kind to Brian and Marie. Strangers in the night as they'd been. We'd all been a bit suspicious too, but we hadn't asked either of them any real questions— even Mum hadn't. But then that wasn't Mum's way. She waits for people to tell her things. She can look foolish but on this occasion she'd been less foolish than most people would have been. It might have seemed mad to have hired a private detective when she did, but now it looked prophetically sane.

Dad at first refused to think about the private detective. He was concentrating on Grace.

"I'll go and see Grace," said Dad, "and shake it out of her."

"Shake what out of her?" said Mum. "I doubt if Grace asked any questions either. Besides she's pregnant," she added reasonably, "about seven months or so now." That gave me a shock. "You can't possibly shake her."

"Maybe not," said Dad reluctantly. "But what else can we do?"

He meant, what are you going to do, Elizabeth? Dad is the bossy one, the recorder of faults, but Mum tends to make the decisions.

"We'll go and see my private detective," said Mum firmly. I could see that she was proud of having a private detective of her very own. "He hasn't had much time to find out anything yet but we'll go and see him and give him a bit of a push and shove. And tell him about Marie. I haven't had time to do that yet. You never know, they may both be crooks."

"Both!" said Dad.

"Well, we all suspected that Brian was a crook. You said yourself that he was on the run," Mum said patiently. "Of course speculating always seems to be different from knowing something. I mean we all read about middle-class crooks these days but somehow we never expect to meet one. Most of our best friends might be crooks," she said thoughtfully, "except that they're not rich enough. I think Brian was a crook and Marie, I don't know about Marie. But we'd better find out. We'll go and see my private detective tomorrow."

"Can I come?" I asked.

"No you can't," said Mum. "Tomorrow you go back to school."

***

CHAPTER EIGHT

T hey call this the spring term. You get up in the dark and put on your reflector belt and bicycle lights before there's a bird stirring and they call that spring. It always seems to me that schools wish your life away as Grandma would say, *did* say, years ago.

"I wish it was next week and my birthday," I'd say.

"You're wishing your life away," Grandma would say.

Schools are going-to-be places. It's always nearly spring, nearly summer, nearly into Inter time, almost Leaving time and before you've got half-way through first year, they're talking about University. Rush, rush, rush. There's no time just to be.

Still, it was good to be back. I've nowhere to go except family and school. Usually I prefer family to school but now, well now, I didn't know. Family life over Christmas had been a bit terrifying and suffocating. Dangerous, really. Dangerous and boring as if something was about to happen and never quite did. Unlike school where any present happening is almost in the past.

It was nice to smell chalk and furniture polish and even the sweaty warm smell of lots of bodies at assembly. It was comforting to see people I hardly knew and didn't care about. Little people in my mind. Everyone at home, Marie included, seemed big. The other thing about school is that there's no atmosphere (except for sweat and chalk). People say what they mean and if they don't say what they mean then no one hears them. At home I've got my ear half-cocked all the time for nuances and silent noises, zings and zangs. At school there's a subdued roar, but it doesn't mean a thing. Unless you ask it to.

I came out of school late, that first day back. I'd loitered around after the bell rang and then I'd had to go and collect some books I'd forgotten from the school library, which meant a long argument about forgetfulness and being inconsiderate with the old bat who was trying to lock it up. By the time I got to the bicycle shed, it was empty, except for my bike and two battered ones which always seemed to be there and must have been left behind by two 1950s ghosts. They're big black bicycles with baskets, one with a cross-bar (for a man), and one without (for a lady). The baskets get more and more shredded every term and I doubt if you could move the bikes now without them falling apart. I sometimes wonder what they're doing there, and who left them behind, and why. Nobody seems to care about them. Did Romeo die, and Juliet, and leave nothing but black bicycles with baskets behind? One of life's little mysteries, as Grandma would say.

My bike was on its side, which was no mystery at all. My bike is small. It has little wheels and an adjustable saddle. It is, for some reason, a target. Most people at school have mountain bikes, or racing bikes. Bikes, in any case, with curved handle-bars and narrow, bum-slicing saddles. They all hate my bike. I think it makes them feel uncomfortable about their own pretentious and useless ones. I mean where do they think they're racing *to*? What mountain can they climb? Dublin traffic is flat and foolish. But often, when I get to the shed, I find my bike on the ground, the adjustable saddle detached. Middle-class vandalism, I call it. But even

Mum, who doesn't know about the vandalism, is embarrassed by my bike. She keeps on offering to buy me a new,
conventional model with curved handlebars, bum-slicing
saddle and every modern inconvenience. I won't let her.
My bike's my bike and I've got to feel about it the way I feel
about my dolls, poor dusty Dragon Lady and all the other
ladies. You have to stand up for a sturdy, useful, little bike
like mine. So I righted the bike and slapped seventeen
pounds of books on the back carrier. I think they weigh
seventeen pounds, the books, because Mum once put them
on the scales with the cat and since she knew the cat's
weight she worked out the book weight. I've never been
too sure about it myself. Mum is not reliable about facts
and figures, particularly not about weight. Or is that Dad
talking?

I was upset and tired and cross about my bike on the
ground so, as I peddled away, I didn't notice, or want to
notice, that the bike felt more wobbly than it usually did.
I was a bit dreamy that day.

And then a car edged in, trying to avoid another car
which was trying to pass it. Dublin drivers like to think
they're demons. They're always trying to stay ahead of each
other so that they can be first in the next traffic jam. The
car hit my shoulder with a th¹⁻k sort of slam, and my
saddle and me parted company from the bike, over and
over, so slowly it was like a dream.

Naturally, the drivers didn't stop, either of them. They
probably muttered something about bad-words cyclists and
rushed for the nearest traffic lights, not looking back.

I felt a bit sick and just lay there. I felt as if I'd like to lie
there for ever and ever and leave the job of putting me and
the bike together again to someone else. I wanted to give

up and not begin to think about the moment when I'd
have to feel angry about the drivers and whoever it was
who thought it was funny to loosen my saddle.

"Are you all right?" said a voice.

It was the Polite Boy.

It's a bit foolish to be found lying on a cold pavement
in the near dark of four-thirty on a spring term afternoon,
(January, yet), with your bike and your books around you
in bits. *I* minded, but The Polite Boy didn't seem to mind
at all. Well, he was like that.

The Polite Boy (No, I didn't think this all out on the
pavement, I knew it already) is an unusual boy. Our school
is a good middle-class school—academically excellent, Mum
says. And that means, as far as I can see, that most of the
people in it are polite in a slightly rude sort of way. Polite
to adults, rude to each other. They drop rubbish all over the
place (including beer cans), and care about the environ-
ment. Their parents pick them up in fast cars and worry
about pollution. They're mostly left-wing, the kids in our
school. Up for prisoners, particularly political ones, and
down on law and order,

The Polite Boy is different. He has a name. He's called
Stephen. Everyone else calls him that except me. When I
talk to him—not often—I call him "You" to his face. But
when I think about him I call him The Polite Boy. He's odd.
He really is. He's up for law and order but not down on
prisoners. He's always saying not-quite-the-right-thing in
RE, class. I mean he won't go along with the latest protest.
He's always sticking up for unlikely people. Sometimes I
think he'd stick up for Judas if he thought Judas was
interesting enough. That's the point about The Polite Boy.
He thinks, but mostly he likes to think against everybody

else.

"I'm sorry," he'd say, not sorry at all. "I don't think that's quite the point. I think violence within a democracy is wrong. If we vote for people, we should respect them."

All this didn't, quite, flash through my mind lying on the pavement on that cold and frightening afternoon. I just knew that I was glad that it was The Polite Boy, and no one else, who had found me there.

"I'm not all right," I said from the pavement. " I was knocked down by a car and my saddle came off and I don't want to get up. I don't want to put it all together again."

"The bike?" said The Polite Boy. "Well, I've got it here and your books too, and your notes, if these scruffy folded-up bits of paper are your notes. And I've found your saddle. I'll screw it on for you again if you like."

"That's very kind of you," I said, getting up and feeling ridiculous because my legs were trembling and most of me was quivering in a strange uncontrolled way. It was as if some giant animal was shaking me by remote control, scary and humiliating.

"Not at all, not at all," squeaked Stephen. He has this high voice which he uses when he wants to be very polite or formal. He leant over me as I stood there shaking and bowed several times in a prayerful manner. "Not at all, anything to be of service."

"Do you always talk like that?" I asked, stumbling against his rather thin torso.

"Almost always," he squeaked. "I think your knees are bleeding," he went on in this other husky voice. "You should wash them. You can't ride your bike. I'll walk you home."

He did too. He screwed on the saddle, secured the books more safely to the back carrier, clutched the bike and said

"Where to?"

"Do you always walk?" I asked for the sake of something to say. It had suddenly occurred to me that The Polite Boy was, in fact, handsome. Odd that. I'd never noticed it at school. Perhaps because the girls at school seem to work on some subliminal hormonal level which means that they're attracted to broad muscular boys in black leather. Macho, I suppose. I don't go for muscle much or black leather either. But when there's a standard, however off the wall it is, everyone tends to accept it. I didn't want to go out with a broad black-leather boy but I did think it was a pity that none of those boys fancied me. They often laughed at Stephen at school because he was almost fanatically formal. If he got a mark on his clothes he'd dab at it for ages with a bit of carefully folded tissue. He didn't wear black or leather or anything hot-looking. He wore the school uniform, scrupulously, but as if it was some kind of esoteric joke. Laughing at the laughers. He'd even bought these fancy braces in the school colours and on St Patrick's Day he wore bright green braces. A different shirt each morning and his tie was always dead centre, neatly knotted and sometimes he embellished it with a tie-pin. Everyone else mangled their ties and wore them under their ears. They all looked the same that way but they thought they were being individual and rebellious and that satisfied them. They never noticed that they were creating their own indignant uniform. Now Stephen really was individual without being indignant and he had bright wings of light brown hair which he tossed back whenever he was talking, well declaiming really. Stephen did a lot of declaiming. I'd watched him, of course, at school. When you're a little on the outside you tend to do a lot of watching but somehow

I had never seen him as himself before. He had been hidden behind a label. Schools do label people because they're brisk, convenient places and labels are brisk convenient things. Once you've got a label, it sticks. So I was Clever Antonia and Stephen was Odd. If I had won Miss Ireland and Stephen had been declared All-Rounder of the Year, I don't suppose it would have made much difference at school. We'd still be stuck by our labels. But here he was, suddenly handsome and here I was, suddenly embarrassed, and I couldn't help thinking that we were both much more interesting than our labels.

"I always walk," said Stephen who was staring at the newly-lit windows of the houses on Palmerston Road as if they fascinated him. "My parents don't have a car."

"Goodness, how odd of them," I said. "Neither do mine. Wouldn't people be shocked if they knew?"

"Horrified," said Stephen. "Not that I care really." I felt he did, a bit. I thought about Dad being a chef and the silly things that matter too much.

"What happened your bike?" said Stephen, "Apart from the car. Since you weren't hurt, how did it come apart like that?"

"Someone unscrewed the saddle in the bike-shed. They don't like my bike at school. It's odd-looking."

"It's a perfectly good bike!" said Stephen indignantly. "It's a very sensible bike. You don't want an unstable thing with curved handle-bars and a wispy, wimpish frame in Dublin traffic. Why *don't* they like it?"

"Well, it looks silly, I suppose. I often feel like an elephant trying to balance on a golf ball on it. It is safe, though, because it's low, and I won't change it."

"You shouldn't *have* to change it," squeaked Stephen,

his hair fairly flying with fury. "If they've been messing about with your bike you should report it. You should tell Mrs Davis. You should tell the headmaster. You should tell your mother. You could have been killed!"

"That's a lot of telling," I said, pleased with his rage. "I don't like telling tales." It was ridiculous because he was right. I could have been killed.

"That's not telling tales. Anyway what's wrong with telling tales? No-one told tales on the Nazis and look what happened then."

"The school isn't fascist Germany."

"The Germans wouldn't admit the holocaust was happening," said Stephen darkly. "They said they didn't know. If something wrong happens you should tell. Tell your mother anyway. Let her tell someone else."

"Mum would be upset."

"Of course she'd be upset. Why shouldn't she be upset? It's her *business* to be upset. I'll tell her if you like. I'll tell her when we get back to your place."

It seemed an astonishing thing to offer. Most boys would run a mile rather than meet somebody's mother and this boy, this really rather amazing boy, was offering not merely to meet Mum but to instruct her as well.

"I'll tell her. You might exaggerate."

"Me? Exaggerate?" his voice rose squeak-wards. "Well I'll come to the door and see that you do tell her."

As it happened Mum was waiting for me. She was peering out the dining-room side window which looked on to the porch when we came through the gate. Ever since my coolness with Grace, Mum has been getting more and more motherly. So there she was, clucking and fussing, before I had a chance to find my key and open the front door.

"You're late, Antonia. What happened? I was *worried*." I think I'd prefer the old unworried Mum. Mum, worried, was just like all the other mothers in the world. You've worried me, she seemed to say.

"Antonia was knocked off her bike," said Stephen in his deep voice and then he squeaked, "Someone interfered with her saddle."

"This is Stephen, Mum. Stephen, this is Mum," I said. Always one for the formalities.

"How did they interfere with your saddle? How can you interfere with a saddle?" Mum frowned at Stephen as if it was his fault.

"They loosened it. It's a sort of joke. They think Antonia's bike is funny, well that's the sort of childish sort of sense of humour they have, so they loosened the saddle but they left it on so that Antonia didn't know it was loose. So when a car knocked against her, she went over."

"Oh my God," said Mum. "Oh Antonia, oh I'm so sorry. Oh look at your poor knees."

"Well, I'll be going then," said Stephen. He was brave enough to instruct anyone, including A Mother, but an Emotional Mother was another thing entirely. I could see that he wanted to run. So very male. I couldn't help being pleased that there was something predictable about him.

"Oh no you don't," said Mum smartly as she pulled him in the door. "You'll come right in here, Stephen, and tell me about it. And Antonia, go upstairs and wash your knees with Dettol."

"That," said Mum an hour later when Stephen had gone, "is a very nice boy." I was sitting at the kitchen table near the fire and my bandaged knees were stinging. I'd washed them and put Savlon on them—Dettol indeed—but Savlon wasn't serious enough for Mum, who had unearthed an incredibly ancient and possibly dangerous elastic bandage and bound my knees formally while Stephen declaimed about irresponsibility and schoolboy humour. They were both playing parts, of course, but I must say I enjoyed it enormously.

"A very nice boy," said Mum. "Why didn't you mention him before?"

"Well I didn't really know him before," I said, loosening Mum's safety pins. They were rusty. "At school they think he's peculiar."

"Your school seems more than a little peculiar to me," said Mum grimly. "That's an expensive middle-class school and they behave like vandals. Fun, *fun* to bully and tease and put your life in danger."

"All schools are like that, Mum," I said. "Most of them are worse. They don't think about danger. If they think it's funny, then you're a spoil-sport if you don't think so too."

"And what do the teachers think?" asked Mum. "Stephen said he thought they'd done this to your bike before. He said he thought you might have complained about it?"

"Well yes I did," I said awkwardly. "I told Mrs. Davis and she said I should report it if it happened again."

"Oh she did, did she?" said Mum. "Well this time I'll report it. I'll write to Mrs. Davis tomorrow. This WILL NOT DO! Still," she said, calming down abruptly, "still, he's a nice boy. I'm glad some good came of it."

I was so busy being an invalid and refusing Mum's offers of various, and probably dangerous, medicaments that I forgot all about Brian and Marie until the next evening. Dad was home, for once, and Mum had gone out to see Grandma who had flu.

"Your mother says he's a nice boy," said Dad, who was sitting in the kitchen listening to music on his special stereo speakers when I cam in.

"Don't tease, Dad," I said. "Anyway, if she's my mother she's your wife. Why don't you use her name? Try calling her EEElizabeth or even Liz, or Lizzie. I know she's my mother. You don't have to tell me."

"Is he a nice boy?" asked Dad.

"Very nice. Don't tease. He's just a boy and he's nice."

"And you're a girl, and you're nice."

"Oh shut up!"

"Your mother, sorry, my wife said not to tease," said Dad. "But I'm glad he's nice."

"He's not important," I said, and felt my face burning.

"Oh no?" said Dad. "Well I'm glad young women can still blush."

I made dinner. Dad is quite hopeless in an ordinary domestic kitchen. He needs Sabatier knives, steel steamers and a blowtorch, truly, a blowtorch, to make any sense of food. I learnt a lot about so-called *haute cuisine* from Dad. They seal meat with a blowtorch before roasting it fast in the very hottest oven. Gratin means scorched and everything about Dad's chef life seems to be dangerous, hot and flaming. He says it makes for good food, but on the whole, he prefers bad food. He prefers overcooked cauliflower to mange-tout peas. He loves white sauce, the thick, milky, floury sort because, he says, he's come to hate Hollandaise and all the ways of preventing it from curdling. He won't let Mum buy a dishwasher or even a washing-machine. He says he prefers a domestic kitchen, calm and quiet and Mum says she does too, so why doesn't he remove the loudspeakers?

I don't make domestic efforts for Dad. I just put two

steak-and-kidney pies and two large potatoes in the oven. I sliced tomatoes and poured bottled dressing over them. Dad loves it.

"Ah, monosodium glutamate," he says, "that glorious commercial taste." He's a food snob in reverse, Dad is. He can't understand why anyone pays to eat in a restaurant.

Dad doesn't talk to me the way Mum does. Mum talks to me the way she'd talk to any adult. Mum uses good words and thinks good thoughts but nothing and no-one is too small for her particular attention. Dad's not like that. I think he loves Mum's gossip and her stories about why the Queen carries a handbag and why our next-door neighbour stood at his front door at four o'clock in the morning and said he couldn't go on. Mum says that she knows all those stories because she learned how to listen to people in Grandma's old kitchen.

"The maids liked me, you see," she said. "We did have maids in those days and they liked me. She never did." She being Grandma. Anyway the maids gave Mum a taste for what Grandma calls "Low Gossip."

"Did you know Mary wants to be cremated?" said Mum the other day. Mary is another neighbour.

"Why?" said Dad.

"Well, she's frightened of worms."

Dad talks to me about music and it's fascinating because when you watch Dad listening to music, you can see him feel the notes. But if you want to find out what the detective said about Brian and Marie, and I did, no good asking Dad.

"What did the private detective say about Brian and Marie, Dad?" I asked.

"Ha!" said Dad nodding his head, bound to the music by a thread that seemed to be pulling his left ear "H'm. Oh

Brian and *Marie*. Nothing much. He said they might be crooks. The Guards are looking for them. Fur coats or something. Listen to this, just listen how he does it," and Dad started conducting with his hands.

"Crooks, Dad? Brian and Marie?"

"Oh yes, credit cards and cheques." said Dad. "But just listen to this."

It was no good. I'd just have to wait for Mum.

And that was no good either, for dear old Grandma, the witch, was worse. She'd neglected her flu (Dad didn't believe this, he thought she was malingering), and stopped taking her antibiotics for the throat infection which followed it and she had, said Mum, a severe bronchial infection that might have been pneumonia. Mum was dead impressed by the seriousness of it all but Dad was sceptical.

"Who said it might-have-been pneumonia? Your mother or the doctor?" asked Dad. "I think she's having a whale of a time, the best she's had since she wore out the excitement of widowhood. It's a pity it wasn't pneumonia. That might have shut her up."

"Oh darling," said Mum. "Don't say that."

Grandma refused to go into hospital. She didn't have private medical insurance (too mean), and she was too posh for a public ward, even if she could get a bed. So poor Mum had to move into Grandma's horrid house in Castleknock and see that she took her antibiotics this time.

"I don't think she wants to get well," said Mum. "She keeps on getting out of bed to feed that nasty smelly cat of hers and she pretends she's taken her antibiotics when she hasn't. The doctor says I'm to keep them and dole them out. The doctor says that she may be getting confused."

"Nonsense," said Dad. "She's as sharp as she ever was.

This is just her way of solving the servant problem."

I was lonely after Mum left. It was a case of wake Dad, feed him at five (he was on dinners at the hotel), and shove him out the door. I missed Mum. I missed talking. I even missed the rows.

And I hadn't been able to go back and see Grace after Marie had left. There was a whole lot of adult stuff there, just waiting for me, Brian and his alumicron suit. Marie wanting a baby. Marie cringing in her fur coat (had it been paid for?) in bed. It was all too much and too little. Too much feeling and too little information.

Instead I sought out Stephen. I saw him every day at school but though he'd been polite in a concerned sort of way about my accident, I didn't know what he thought about me or whether he liked me or not. He had seemed to like me. But he wasn't a planning sort of boy. If he liked a girl, he'd wait for fate to bring him near her. Well, that's what I told myself and I comforted myself with some of Mum's more remarkable stories about how she courted Dad. Sleeping pills in the coffee and a clock that she kept changing so that, lo and behold, one minute it was early and the next it was far too late to catch the last bus so Dad had to stay the night in Mum's flat instead of going home to his own mum. Dad says that he knew what she was up to, she was never very good at crushing sleeping pills. Dad says he played along because he liked her and that after all he did marry her, didn't he? Mum says that most men give in to strong-minded women.

"He only got to like me later."

I didn't want to repeat Mum's mistakes. I mean I didn't really want to lure Stephen, but what can you do if you think someone would like you if they only gave themselves the chance? I liked Stephen. Therefore he must like me a little, musn't he? It wasn't sex I was thinking of. Most of the time I try not to think about sex. I was thinking about friendship and about the good feeling I'd had when Stephen was walking along beside me, down Palmerston Road, talking about doors and Dublin architecture. Stephen seems to be fascinated by Dublin architecture.

"Stephen," I said one day at lunch when I came across him accidentally-on-purpose in the canteen, "Stephen, how would you like to see an intact example of an Irish Urban Garden of the last century? The garden has long twisted terracotta ropes to edge the paths and there's cinders for drainage." I wasn't making a very good fist of this. Just repeating things I'd heard Dad say but then Stephen was a bit like Dad. More interested in doors than in people. "There's a house too, an early Victorian-Georgian one with a huge round-headed window."

"Who lives there?" said Stephen suspiciously. I could see that he was thinking I was a vamp. "Your house is Edwardian fake-Tudor."

"Yes, well, I know *that*," I said. "But this house is different. It's in flats, propped up with girders. It's a nearly dead house but somehow it's still alive. It does have a garden and my Aunt Grace lives in the top flat. Under the roof. If you use the sink, you get tea-leaves in the bath."

"A round-headed window?" said Stephen.

"Yes," I said, "most definitely a round-headed window. It lights up the whole hall." And the tired old scratched wallpaper and the worn lino on the stairs. But I didn't say that.

"I'd like to see your aunt's house," said Stephen politely, "if you'd arrange it and let me know. Perhaps you could phone me?"

"Do you have a card?" I asked.

"A card?" said Stephen, looking puzzled.

"A card with your telephone number on it, and your address and function in life. Clearly this is a business appointment. Maybe your secretary could get back to mine?"

And then Stephen laughed. "You sound like my Mum. She says that when I'm invited out somewhere social, I behave as if I'd been promised a trip to the most sadistic dentist in town. I just don't like going places I've never been or meeting people I've never met. It's a waste of time. I'd prefer to stay at home and read a book."

"Well how can you know that it's a waste of time if you don't try it?" I said priggishly. The trouble was that I understood him. Usually I felt the same way myself. Books are easier than people. At least you can choose your own books and they won't be hurt, or feel offended, if you put them down and sit, dreaming out of the window, in their presence. Books don't have to understand you. You have to understand them, but they won't know if you couldn't be bothered to try.

"I like doing things on my own," said Stephen. "I like foreign places when I get there—but I'm always travel-sick on the way."

"Well, it's not far on foot to Aunt Grace's and you can't get sick on foot," I said. "But don't come if you don't want to. I just thought you'd be interested," I added in my best imitation of Grandma's Hurt Voice, a winner every time.

"I am, I am interested," said Stephen and just before school was over he handed me a card, labelled A Very Elaborate Calling Card. It was a thing of beauty. It was edged with celtic curlicues which reminded me of Dad's

Christmas tree-stand. Stephen had written his name in fine black ink, more curls, Elizabethan underlinings this time, I thought. Squiggle, squiggle. At the bottom of the card (which was, in fact a folded sheet of A4 typing paper) he'd put his telephone number in huge figures. And then he'd added in his ordinary, half-print handwriting. "Please phone. This executive won't be too busy to take your call. Love (Did he mean love?), Stephen Gibson."

And that meant that I'd have to see, meet, forgive? Aunt Grace. Forgive or be forgiven. It's all the same thing in our family. And that meant that I'd have to go and see Mum in Grandma's horrid house in Castleknock and find out about Brian and Marie.

❦❦❦

CHAPTER NINE

Mum was taking Grandma's mouldy cat out of the washing-machine when I arrived in Castleknock. Grandma's house is called "The Larches" by Grandma and 13 Oaktown Glebe by everybody else. Grandma's address infuriates Dad.

"Well, where are these larches? There isn't a larch in sight and where are the oaks that make the glebe? What is a glebe anyway?"

"Oh shut up," said Mum who is always embarrassed by Grandma's sillier snobberies. "Look it up in the dictionary since you're so clever."

We just call Grandma's house Castleknock or Her place and go pale when we think of it. It is, truly, the most horrid house. It's a seventies imitation Georgian house which looks like something a child might have assembled out of neo-vernacular building blocks, Dad says. The handles spring out of the doors if you slam them and there are fake cornices and confused-looking fireplaces with liver marble surrounds and wicked little brass knobs placed here and there in a pointless sort of way. "Ten styles for a single price," says Dad. "And none of them genuine." I don't care much about style or architecture but there is something dreadful about Grandma's house. Everything is light and bright and low-looking. The furniture is velvet and tiny. There are no bookshelves and no books, which gives the rooms a strange bare look. "A parlour look," Mum calls it. "Just for show—

not living in." It's like a terrible doll's house with wall-to-wall carpeting and no soul. There is bottle-glass beside the front door and a big picture-window with patio doors in the big room at the back. Grandma calls this the dining-room though, as far as I know, no one has ever been invited to dine. There's a little mean kitchen area divided by a counter from the dining-room. Anything functional or friendly in the kitchen is hidden from curious public eyes by woody-looking doors which squeak when you open them. You can never find a pot or pan. But then Grandma doesn't do much cooking. Underneath the antique-effect woodery is the real business of the kitchen, the gleaming white machines, dishwasher, washing-machine, and clothes-dryer. It's a schizoid kitchen really, half-practical, half-dream and wholly nasty because it's all pretence. Grandma has parquet in the dining room and tile-effect lino in the kitchen area. I think she thinks cooking is a bit rude.

I came around the back and through the patio doors which weren't locked, and peered over the counter because I knew I'd find Mum in the kitchen. She always prefers a kitchen, no matter how horrible, to any other room.

And there was Mum, dear Mum, crouched in front of the washing-maching taking out the cat.

"It could do with a wash," I said, trying to blink my tears away, I was suddenly so very pleased to see her. "It's a very grubby cat."

"It's a disgusting cat, Antonia," said Mum and stood up. I was shocked, really shocked. She'd got so thin. Her jeans were hanging off her and her skin was stretched and white. It was only ten days since I'd last seen Mum. How could she have lost so much weight in ten days?

"What's the cat doing in the washing-machine, Mum?"

I asked.

"Hiding," said Mum. "This cat likes to cringe whenever I come near it and then when it's finished cringing, it goes and hides, usually in the washing-machine though it has tried the dryer as well. It's a constant temptation to me. What if I pretended I hadn't noticed and turned the washing-machine on with the cat inside? Oh well." Mum stretched and the jeans slipped further. The cat cringed and trembled in the corner. I could see what Mum meant. All that cringing and trembling made you want to kick it. Was that what Grandma felt with Mum? Unbrearable thought. Anyway Grandma had created Mum's cringing. Neither of us had done anything to the wretched cat.

"How's Grandma?" I asked.

"Worse, better, I don't know," said Mum, striding through to the dining area and opening the patio doors. "I'm going to have a cigarette," she said defiantly.

"Go ahead," I said in some amazement. "When did I ever try to stop you?"

"Grandma makes me smoke outside. She says it's a filthy habit. Well it is, it is. But she asks me to look after her and then she orders me about and I feel so childish and silly when I'm with her, cringing like the cat."

"Oh Mum," I said. "You're not silly."

"No," said Mum who had found the most remarkable ashtray on the sideboard. It was a greenish marble and it had this great big shiny silver lighter attached to its rim. Typical Grandma. She wouldn't let Mum smoke but she did provide an all-in-one smoking machine—for guests.

"Does she have a silver cigarette box with stale cigarettes in it too?" I asked, "Just in case An Important Man might come to call?"

Mum, who was puffing desperately out through the patio doors, turned and smiled.

"How did you know? She does, she does."

"I'm going to see Grace," I said, "I thought I'd tell you this time. I thought I'd bring Stephen with me because he likes old houses. And he might make it easier, seeing Grace."

"And I thought you came to see me because you missed me," said Mum. I stared at her. Self-pity was most unlike Mum.

"*Mum*, Mum, stop it. Of course I did. I wanted to talk to you about Grace and ask about Brian and Marie too. I need your advice. There's nothing wrong with being useful, you know."

"Isn't there?" said Mum. "I'm sorry, Antonia. I'm so glad you came. I just feel helpless and stuck and there's something about this house that reminds me of constant Sunday afternoons in the suburbs with nothing to look forward to after a very heavy lunch. I hate being useful!" And she slammed the patio doors together.

"Well, try hating Grandma then," I said huffily. "Don't take it out on me."

"Sometimes I'd like to strangle her," said Mum, dreamily picking at the cellophane on her cigarette packet, "and then she starts coughing and reaches for my hand and I know that she's frightened of dying, and she squeezes my hand, and squeezes it, and she's coughing and coughing and I can't hate her but I do hate her because she's squeezing my life away."

"Don't let her, Mum. You don't owe her anything. She could afford a private nursing home. You should be ruthless."

"I'm not good at being ruthless," said Mum. "I don't

even want to be." It was true. Grandma bullied Mum in a bad way and Dad bullied her in a good way and Mum fought both of them from time to time but there was a thin little determined strand of innocence in Mum which neither of them could touch. It wasn't even a fighting matter. No one could force her to do something she thought was wrong, or, more usually, force her not to do something she thought was right.

"I once told a friend of mine that I wanted to be good," Mum told me years ago, "and she burst out laughing. She thought it was funny, wanting to be good. I've hated her ever since, which is not good, but I still want to be good."

It was rather fine, if infuriating. Do as you would be done by rather than do as you have been done to. The trouble was, it seemed to me, that Mum simply couldn't keep it up. And then I thought of Mum wanting to eliminate the cat and Mum wanting to strangle Grandma and I giggled.

"Your imagination's ruthless," I said. "Strangling Grandma and putting the cat through a full cycle. Anyway," I said because I could see that the thought of her ruthless imagination was bringing a little pleased flush to Mum's cheeks, "anyway, what about Brian and Marie? What did the private detective say?"

"Well," said Mum, "he said they were the most dis-organised pair of crooks he'd ever come across."

"Really?" I asked. "Really crooks?"

"Almost crooks. I don't know much about the law," admitted Mum. "Brian's a sort of professional womaniser or an amateur who makes womanising his profession. You wouldn't think it, would you, to look at him? He takes up with rich women and then invites them to put money into some scheme he says he has going. Sometimes it's a charity.

Charity! Brian! And sometimes it's a company. Meanwhile he proposes marriage and talks about having children and really there do seems to be a lot of foolish women about because they never seem to check him out or ask about the company or the charity. They just write him personal cheques (to avoid tax, Brian explains) and then Brian takes the money and after a few weeks or months, he leaves, moves on. He does a lot of travelling."

"What about Marie?" I asked.

"Mr Tynan," Mr Tynan was the private detective, "Mr Tynan wasn't too sure about Marie," said Mum. "It's all very small-time—whatever that means. I mean Brian never actually sets up companies or invites more than one person to invest in him at a time. Mr Tynan said he thought that most of the women knew there was no company or charity. They just paid to keep him and they never try to have him prosecuted or anything. But he is in trouble with the law. He tends to leave a long line of bouncing checks behind him. He bought a fur coat in Dublin before Christmas and the cheque he used to pay for that bounced."

"Well, Marie did need a new fur coat," I said. "Her old one was a bit ratty and perhaps she didn't know what Brian was up to. Did Mr Tynan think she was in on it?" All this talk about crooks was beginning to make me talk like a member of the Famous Five. Any second now and I'd ask for ginger pop.

"Marie, Mum?" I asked. I didn't mind if Brian was a crook but I'd liked Marie.

"Marie," said Mum, "Marie tends to come along after Brian has left. It might be some weird form of marriage by proxy or love by remote control. I mean Marie doesn't get to spend much time with Brian so maybe she wants to enjoy his love affairs in retrospect. That's what I think. Mr Tynan thinks it's a kind of benign blackmail. A woman who has been fooled by Brian might feel sorry for Marie and not prosecute, however angry she was. But that doesn't seem right to me since Mr Tynan is convinced that women never mean to prosecute anyway."

"It sounds very ugly to me," I said slowly, thinking about liking Marie and about the things she'd said to me, which must be, I knew, untrue. She'd talked about Brian being one of nature's more willing victims but it was Brian's women who were the victims, not Brian.

"Yes, it does sound very ugly," said Mum. "But even if Mr Tynan is right about Marie, you must remember that Marie might be just as much a victim as the other women. Anyway being crooked doesn't necessarily mean that you're false in everything. And I think she did like you, Antonia. I think that was real."

"But why Grace?" I asked. I felt like hugging Mum for being so nice but somehow I knew that Mum didn't want to be hugged just now. All that squeezing was making her untouchable. "Grace isn't rich."

"Oh Grace, Grace," said Mum sounding just like Grandma. "Who can explain Grace? Why did she go for him? Why did he go for her? I don't know. Mr Tynan said that Brian might have thought that Grace was rich and then found out that she wasn't."

"He couldn't have thought that," I said sadly, thinking of Grace's flat, the nicest, most un-rich-looking place I'd ever been in. I was beginning to think that Mr Tynan must be rather stupid. "Grace doesn't even look rich."

"No she doesn't," agreed Mum. "Perhaps he fell in love with her. There is something about Grace, and even inefficient crooks must fall in love sometimes. Besides, both Brian and Marie, well, each of them seems to have had a serious fantasy about having a baby. They're both quite odd enough to think they could turn fantasy into reality. Brian stole affection and money from women who fell in love with him. Perhaps he thought he could steal a baby as well." Mum sat down at the dining-room table and started to polish the marble ashtray with a little piece of scrunched up tissue she took out of her jeans pocket. She sprinkled stale, light ash across the yards of polished wood.

"Mum, you can't really think that!"

"Can't I?" said Mum. "You have to remember what sort of lives they lead. They're used to playing parts and acting fantasies. I think if you lived like that long enough you'd come to believe that you could get anything you wanted just by pretending it was true. I want, therefore I have. It's a sad story. The saddest thing is that they never seem to get rich, Brian and Marie. I mean I don't like crooks but there's something quite terrifying about crooks who live in constant fear and exile. They're quite powerless really. Perhaps that's why Brian needed to believe he wanted Grace and this absurd baby," said Mum, sounding annoyed again. Mum often sounded annoyed these days when she talked about Grace. "Grace has her own security. You wouldn't find her in Castleknock looking after a half-mad cat and a vengeful old woman."

"Mum," I said, "you don't have to feel sorry for crooks. You don't even have to feel not sorry for Grace. You might try getting angry instead,"

"Angry," said Mum thoughtfully. "I feel angry all the time now but I can't feel angry with Grandma because she's ill and I hate her and I can't feel angry with Brian and Marie because they're pathetic. I do feel angry with Grace because she's not here and I am. Most of all, I feel angry with myself for being such a wimp. I feel sick with anger with myself," Mum said, "because I am such a wimp."

At this point there was a dainty ting-a-ling from upstairs.

"What's that, Mum?"

"That's Grandma's cowbell. She wants something," said Mum. "You stay down here, I'll see if she wants to see you."

Grandma did want to see me. She also wanted, Mum said, tea with lemon and no milk on the Chinese lacquer tray—no tray-cloth because Mum didn't launder the tray-cloths properly. All this at the tinkle of a cowbell.

"And don't say anything witty about cowbells," said Mum as she scuttled frantically around the kitchen. "You just go and keep her quiet."

Grandma was sitting up in bed with a pink crochet shawl over her bony shoulders. She was playing patience on a big lacquer tray, the grandfather version of the small one on which Mum was to place the China tea. It was a light, hot, pink room. The central heating was on but Grandma also had an electric fire which glared towards the bed. There was a pink satin quilt on the bed, no duvet for Grandma, and pink pillows.

The carpet was pink and so were the velvet curtains and even the net curtains behind the velvet ones. The lampshades were pink. Everything was pink except Grandma, who was a kind of waxy yellow.

"Antonia," said Grandma. "You've come to see me at last."

"Actually I came to see Mum," I said impatiently because all the pink heat was making me cross.

"Oh," said Grandma. Click, click, clickedy click went

the quiet cards.

"Mum's looking tired."

"You may sit down," said Grandma. I looked around and found a sort of pink box in the corner. There were no chairs. Well, who'd want to sit with Grandma?

"Here's the tea," said Mum cheerily, stumbling into the room. "Can you take away the card tray, Antonia?"

"Careful, careful," said Grandma as I seized her tray. "You'll disturb the cards. You're just like your mother, so careless, so impetuous, and why didn't you use a tray-cloth, EEElizabeth? I always like a well-laundered tray-cloth." Mum sighed and settled the tea-tray on Grandma's knees.

"You said I wasn't to use a tray-cloth because I didn't launder them properly."

"Ah yes, well this will just have to do. Pour the tea, pour the tea. Do you expect me to do it myself?"

I sat back on the pink box and put my head against the pink wall. I was suddenly stunned with sleepiness, the sort of sleepiness, overwhelming, alarming, insistent, that I sometimes feel in the back of someone's car. Not that I often sit in cars but when I do, they tend to make me feel panicky with sleep.

"...It won't be long now Antonia and then you can have your mother back." Grandma was talking and had been talking, I suspected, for some time.

"Hm?" I said sitting up. "Oh. Good. I'm very glad to hear that." Mum, who was sitting on the floor—there was nowhere else to sit—suddenly spluttered. She stood up, staggered, as if dizzy and said "Say goodbye, Antonia, to Grandma," in this breathless voice as if she was trying not to laugh. Grandma looked like thunder.

"You'd better go now," said Mum. "If you want to be

home before dark."

"Well, what did I do?" I asked Mum in the hall. "What did I say?"

"Grandma said that she wasn't long for this world. She said it wouldn't be long now and then you looked at her so solemnly and you said, you said," whimpered Mum who was leaning against the wall giggling helplessly, tears streaming down her face, "you said, 'oh good, you were very glad to hear that.' "

Well I was glad I'd offended Grandma, however accidentally, I thought as I walked up our street in the dark, but that didn't solve the problem. I'd have to talk to Dad.

"Dad," I said when I got home, "Dad, I want to talk to you without the stereo. I want you to turn it off and sit down where you're sitting at the kitchen table and listen to me and don't decide that you have a few little repair jobs to do before, during or after. Just listen to me, Dad. It's urgent."

Dad looked up from his paper. "That sounds very intriguing, Antonia. Can I just wait until the end of this movement? Just a few more minutes?" said he, waving his hands in time to the music.

"No, now," I said, and went into the dining-room where the amplifier was and turned the switch to off. There was a deafening silence and I felt quite sad at the sight of Dad's disappointed face. Still, being sorry for people never got anything done.

"It's about Mum," I said. "She's worn out looking after Grandma, and she's got thin and nervy and Grandma's not all that ill anyway. Grandma's not a bit grateful and Mum's really frightened of her. She smokes out the window and listen for cowbells and Grandma sits there playing patience in that horrid pink room and complains that Mum doesn't launder the tray-cloths properly."

"I bet she doesn't," said Dad, grinning. "I bet she uses them as dusters, poor Lizzie."

"Well that's not the point, Dad," I said. "Anyway Mum's not poor, at least she wouldn't be poor if she had someone to stand up for her. She has a sense of duty, that's all."

"And she needs someone to stop her," said Dad. "Is that what you're saying, Antonia? You're saying that I should tell your mother, sorry, Liz, to stop doing her duty to Grandma and come home to do her duty to me. Is that it? *Is* it, Antonia?"

"Well yes," I said, though, put like that, it wasn't quite what I did mean. "You don't even phone Mum at Grandma's."

"And do you know why that is?" said Dad in this even, quiet, furious voice. He was stiff with anger. "Do you know why? It's because the phone at Grandma's is beside her bed and she won't let Liz, your mother, my wife, use the extension downstairs to make private calls home. Or receive them. I am not going to speak to my wife while that bitch is listening. And Liz says she feels uncomfortable phoning me in front of her mother. Well, that's her problem. I don't want her to look after Grandma, who has quite enough money to hire ten nurses if she wanted to. If your mother wasn't there, Grandma *would* have to hire a nurse, or go into a nursing home, or, more probably, get better. Liz knows all that and it infuriates me, really infuriates me, that she allows herself to be used in this pointless way. If she wants to be rescued, she'll just have to rescue herself."

"It's not that Mum doesn't have guts," I said slowly. "It's just that she's so afraid of Grandma. She's like a different person there."

"Yes," said Dad briskly. "So why go there? Why not just say 'No, I can't come and look after you but I'll find you a nurse.' "

"Well, that *sounds* reasonable, Dad, but Mum just can't say that kind of thing."

"I think she can, you know," said Dad.

❦

The next day was Wednesday, half-day at school, and when I cycled up the street at half-past one, there was Mum, in a posh grey suit which I'd never seen before, struggling out of a taxi. And I do mean struggle. Little white plastic bags dangled from each of her fingers as she fought to control her dear old green leather shoulder-bag which was heaving around on the ground. The taxi driver was unloading large black plastic sacks from the boot of the car. Mum's designer luggage. She always did travel in style.

But she was back, she was very back, wonderfully back. When I raced upstairs to tell Dad who was listening to Radio 3 in bed, he skipped his full dressing, tooth-brushing and shaving routine and fairly tumbled, well, tripped daintily, downstairs in his black kimono and black leather slippers and hugged Mum at the front door amidst the white plastic bags and the black plastic sacks in front of any neighbour who would care to watch.

"You're back," said Dad.

"You're bristly," said Mum.

"Did you pay the taxi?" asked Dad.

"No I didn't," said Mum. "I put it on Grandma's account." Wonderful, really.

❦❦❦

CHAPTER TEN

"Ah well. It just goes to show you," said Stephen. We were on our way to Grace's flat on a bitterly cold Saturday afternoon. I was wheeling my bike which I wouldn't need on the journey there or back but wheeling a bike seemed a nice safe thing to do when walking with what Grandma would call "a young man." I looked at Stephen. He was a young man. I felt almost painfully girlish beside him.

"It just goes to show you what?" I asked.

"Such are the ways of the world," proclaimed Stephen. "Strange though they may be. We will not see their like again."

"And what's that got to do with Grace or Brian or me either for that matter? In fact what's it got to do with *anything*?"

"Nothing at all," said Stephen sweetly, looking straight ahead. "It's just my way of not talking. I don't know what to say, you see."

"Oh," I said and we progressed silently over the bridge and down the canal.

Perhaps I shouldn't have told him or tried to tell him the sad, involved saga of Grace and Brian and Marie but I didn't know quite what to talk to him about. I don't know anything about architecture or Georgian doors and Stephen seemed, in some ways, so certain of himself and everything around him that it was easy to assume that he'd understand about people too. And now I felt foolish because I'd told him when he clearly didn't want to know. And I felt wrong as if by telling him I'd somehow betrayed Grace before he'd even met her. But when I was talking to him it hadn't felt like betrayal. I had just told him to try to explain Grace and why this visit was bound to be awkward. Perhaps betrayal begins with someone else's reactions. How was Stephen to know that my heart was pure?

"It's a remarkable story," said Stephen. "It's just that I don't know any of these people. I simply don't know what to say."

"Well don't say anything then," I said snappily. "Keep quiet for once."

"I was trying to keep quiet," replied Stephen, "In my own conversational way." He was quite unperturbed, totally unmoved by my anger.

Mum once said that everyone in our family lives on their nerve-ends and I had this picture in my mind of us all creeping around like caterpillars on these thready, hairy, black little nerve ends. But, she explained, we are a family of women. "Grandma, Grace, you, me," said she, counting on her fingers which is, I think, the only way she can count. Women, she went on, expected to be insulted and therefore they see an insult where none was intended.

"What I mean is," she said, "is that if Dad says my make-up is messy, I think he's saying he doesn't love me."

"But your make-up is always messy," I said.

"Yes I know," she said. "And when he says it is, I react as if he's saying he doesn't love me. And of course that annoys him. So if he goes on saying my make-up is messy and I keep on reacting that way, then he gets irritated and I know he doesn't love me."

"Well why don't you stop wearing make-up then, Mum?" I asked. Mum got very annoyed at that point and said that that wasn't, quite, the idea she was pursuing. Her make-up, she announced, laser-beam eyes flashing, was not germane to the issue. The point was, she said, that if she'd said yes dear, my make-up is messy, then Dad wouldn't have got annoyed and the whole argument would have stayed an argument about make-up. But when she brought love into it, and suspected all sorts of other possible insults, then the insults came as sure as night follows day. "Self-fulfilling prophecies," said Mum. "Men don't expect insults, so they don't tend to react to something that is less than an insult. Women expect insults everywhere. And of course, if a woman said my make-up was messy," said Mum darkly, "I'd know what she meant."

I began to understand what Mum had been trying to say as I watched Stephen's calmness now. The little irritations of somebody's else's anger about something else had no effect on him. He listened to words. He didn't listen for secret attacks on him. Mum often insists that I'm much more confident than she is but I knew, as I walked down by the canal on that February day, that that wasn't quite true. I was my mother's daughter, all right. I kept on listening for the insult behind the words.

"Or the feeling," Mum had said, "We all listen for insults because we expect men to feel as we do."

We being women.

"Men," Mum had added, "usually mean, or think they mean, just what they say. Never ask a man what he means. Unless of course you want him to say more than he thinks, or knows, he means. That's dangerous. Men don't like straying into unknown emotional territory. If you ask a man more than he thinks or knows he means, he gets aggressive."

Mum's sexist remarks about Men, with a Capital M. But there was a tiny bit of truth in it. If Stephen had been rude to me the way I'd just been rude to him I'd have felt hurt, rejected and insulted. After all I'd felt hurt, rejected and insulted by his much milder remarks.

I looked at him. He was shivering and crouching into his anorak as he tried to pull up the hood.

"What's the matter?" I asked. Perhaps rudeness had a profound physical effect on him.

"It's raining," he said. "I'm going to get soaked."

"That's not rain," I said. "It's just drizzle."

"It's *sleet*!" said Stephen furiously. "I'll probably get pneumonia."

I doubt if he even noticed the homesick garden though I did try to interest him in the cinder space outside the mews and the curved garden paths with their red twisted edgings.

"See, they look like twisted rope," I said. "I wonder who thought of edging paths in that way. It's a bit like acorns on the end of the strings for blinds or pineapples on the tops of walls beside gateways. Why pineapples or acorns or twisted worms for that matter?"

"I'm wet, Antonia," said Stephen, holding his trousers by the knees to prevent them touching the long grass which was spilling over onto the paths. "I'm wet. Does this house have an inside by any chance?"

So we went over the walkway and up through the house, which was, I must admit, looking very shabby. The hall walls are painted in a gloomy shiny gooseberry sludge colour up to waist level and above that there's this very thin yellow-

and-white-patterned wallpaper with medallions on it. The wallpaper has worn through in places and been torn in others; strips of it hung rather drearily in the cold dank air.

"The house doesn't have central heating," I said.

"I can feel that it doesn't," said Stephen.

Even the round-headed window was a disappointment. Stephen looked through it with a shudder.

"It's still sleeting," he said with a shiver.

"Really Stephen, you are a bit wet."

"Yes," he said with a brilliant smile. "That's just what I was trying to tell you. I'm very wet."

Aunt Grace must have heard us coming. She was standing at the top of the stairs, dressed in a patchwork smock. The layers had gone and she'd grown her hair and piled it up on the top of her head. She looked bizarre and magnificent. The patchwork twinkled with tiny mirrors and her skin looked darker. She was also enormous. I mean her stomach was enormous. The rest of her looked slighter and frailer but she had this great taut bump in the middle. She looked like a pregnant woman should look and not the way most of them do look. She hadn't spread sideways. She just sort of billowed.

"Goodness," said Stephen. "Is that your Aunt Grace?"

"Antonia, how lovely to see you," said Aunt Grace, "And this is Stephen."

I'd forgotten how forgiving Aunt Grace could be. She'd been abrupt to surly on the phone and I'd felt guilty because I hadn't seen her or tried to see her for so long. I'd thought that she was trying to punish me. But now I remembered that Aunt Grace always was abrupt on the phone, no matter who was on the other end. She just hated phones. But she didn't bear grudges and she didn't have the sort of tit-for-tat attitude to friendship that some people have.

So now she hugged me to the bump and smiled and hugged me again.

"Oh Antonia, how wonderful to see you." Stephen hummed in the background, an uncomplaining, slightly embarrassed sound and Grace released me and allowed Stephen to bow over her hand before she escorted us into the flat. The flat, I was glad to see, was quite unchanged. It was slightly tidier but it still looked amateurish, not like a real professional home but more like a lair, or, as Grace once pointed out, a student flat.

"I've lived here for more of my life than I care to mention," she'd once said, "But I still think of this place as temporary. I've never been able to buy carpets or curtains, so I just make do with what was here already and cover everything with something else."

When the sag-bag had started to leak polystyrene balls, Grade had mended it with a darning needle and covered the resulting cobbled mess with a large batik hanging which she took down off the wall. She didn't have vases. She put any flowers she picked in an old brown coffee pot but the flat, though eccentric, was a good place to be. It looked as if it belonged to someone. Lots of proper houses look as if they belong to an interior decorator.

Stephen ambled round the flat peering at the books and the huge bunch of dried fennel branches which Grace had put in the corner tied up with string and then forgotten. He seemed uneasy. He had clasped his hands behind his back and he was wandering around in a slightly stooped sort of way as if the ceiling was too low for him. He'd stopped shivering, though, and he'd taken off his anorak and hung it one one of the chairs beside the table in front of the window. The flat was warm, if smelly. Grace, naturally, didn't have central heating. Either she lit a real fire or she used a paraffin contraption that tended to die down from time to time and exude black clouds.

"At least it means that I can't have potted plants. Whenever anyone gives me a potted plant I put it near the paraffin fire and it dies in no time at all."

That had shocked me more than anything else that Aunt Grace had ever told me. Our house is covered with plants, tall figs, wandering swiss cheeses, trembling spiders and Mum loves them all and talks to them. "There pet," she says when she takes off their dead leaves. "There, that feels better now, doesn't it?" She's half laughing at herself when she talks to the plants but she means it just the same. And no, I don't love plants. I dislike the slight smell of decay they give off when they're watered but I don't hate them either. And I couldn't, simply couldn't, kill one deliberately.

"Would you like to see the roof, Stephen?" asked Grace, who'd been clattering in the kitchen. She'd told me she'd give us tea and I was wondering what that would be like.

"The roof?" asked Stephen.

"Yes, the roof. You can climb out onto the roof from the kitchen. There's a wonderful view. You can see for miles up there. To Howth, practically. Antonia says you're very interested in architecture. Well you can see plenty of buildings from up there."

"It's, um, sleeting," said Stephen. "And it'll be getting dark soon. Wouldn't it be dangerous?"

"Nonsense," said Grace firmly and she can sound firmer than Mum. "Nonsense. It's stopped sleeting, the sun's trying to come out and it won't be dark for an hour. Besides, I want to talk to Antonia."

"Well, I could go home then," said Stephen. "I don't want to be in the way."

"You can't go home until you've paid a proper visit and had your tea," said Grace briskly. "Anyway I want to talk to you too. And you won't be in the way if you're on the roof."

I thought it was rather cruel to be quite as direct and unconventional as that to poor Stephen but he didn't seem to mind. He grinned and put his anorak on again.

"Show me how to get up there then. It might be better than the smell from that thing," and he nodded at the belching paraffin fire.

"He's a nice boy, Antonia," said Grace when, with the help of a bit of heaving and pushing and a kitchen chair, we'd dispatched Stephen to the roof. "Brave, funny, I like him."

"Everybody likes him," I said, slightly bitterly because I was getting a bit tired of this universal goodwill. "The point is does he like me?"

"Oh I think so," said Grace. "He only looks at you when you're not looking at him and then he looks quite a lot. And I don't think he'd come on a visit to a very pregnant and unmarried aunt if he didn't like you. I am glad to see you. I've missed you. More than I've missed anyone else. I felt quite cut off without you."

"Well," I said, "you could have phoned. You could have answered the phone. You could have explained about Brian. You missed meeting Marie too. She's his wife. She'd be quite nice if she wasn't married to him. You could have done a lot of things but instead, you just, well, you just hid and left everything, everything from Marie to Grandma, to Mum."

"What about Grandma?" said Grace.

"She's been ill or pretending. Pretending, Dad says. Mum had to go to Castleknock to look after her. Dad was furious and then Grandma and Mum had a row about something I said. And Mum decided that Grandma would just have to pay for a nurse of her own, because, Mum said, she wasn't listening to insults about me from that old witch."

It was oddly boring reciting this. Can words cover events? If Grace had been part of it we could have shared it and discussed it but I couldn't go back and make Grace live it the way we'd lived it. She'd chosen to cut herself off.

"It's all been hard on Mum and she hasn't complained, not much anyway, but it doesn't seem fair to me. I mean she's been left to cope with Brian and Marie and Grandma while you hid. You can't just shut a door and make them all go away. They go on being and annoying other people, Mum, for instance, even if you won't pay a blind bit of attention."

I hadn't realised how angry I was, how unjust I thought it all was, until I started talking. Strangely enough the old rush of affection for Grace had triggered my outburst. I couldn't help that sudden surge of joy I'd felt when I saw her. I couldn't stop the resentment, now, either.

"Yes, I see," said Grace sitting down on a bentwood chair by the table. She stared out through the nursery bars on the window and contemplated the sky.

"The point is you don't seem to see. What are you going to do with that baby when you have it? Heave it up on the roof when it's in the way? Shut the door when it starts crying? You can't hide from a baby, you know."

"Perhaps that's why," said Grace who didn't seem at all disturbed by my rage. I wished she had been. "I knew I'd have the baby for the rest of my life one way or another. And I do like being on my own, having my own time. I just couldn't face being with other people while I was waiting. Though I would have welcomed your company, you know." She turned from the window and smiled at me brilliantly. It sounds like a cliché, I know but Aunt Grace's smile makes her face sparkle with laughter. It truly is a brilliant thing. "I kept telling myself when I was frightened, I kept saying to myself, 'Perhaps this baby won't be an intruder at all. It might be like Antonia. A friend.' That's why I missed you so much when I didn't miss anyone else. That's why."

At this point there was a crash from above.

"Oh my God!" I said. "He's fallen off the roof."

"No he hasn't," said Grace. "It's this side, the noise, and he hasn't passed the window. He's probably slipped on the roof and fallen into the valley. We'd better get him down."

Stephen's face was peering down into the kitchen when we got there.

"I'm very sorry," he squeaked. "I think I've taken a few slates off your roof. It's started sleeting again, snowing really, and I was in a hurry so I slid and then there was this crash."

"Oh that's all right," said Grace. "The roof's the landlord's responsibility. I'll tell him it was a cat burglar and insist that he makes the place more secure. He won't make the place more secure but he will pay for the slates. He's very fond of repairing that roof, my landlord."

Tea was an efficient affair. The paraffin fire had settled down and was now glowing brightly. Grace opened a window, briefly, to get rid of the fumes. She'd bought a chocolate layer cake and a new teapot. Milk was in a jug though she'd only managed a saucer for the sugar. Stephen reclined on the sag-bag and declaimed. He told Aunt Grace about my accident on the bike. He gave his views on cars, illegal carparks, the destruction of Dublin and the way that people, who should know better, called Victorian architecture, Georgian. Someone, he told us, had written an article which said that Collins Barracks were built in 1702 in the reign of King George III. Could we believe that? Grace and I looked blank but it turned out that King George III hadn't come to the throne until 1760, 1760, for heaven's sake, said Stephen as if this was a matter of life and death.

"Does it matter all that much?" asked Grace. She was looking at Stephen's flushed face.

"Matter? Well of course it matters," shouted Stephen. His voice can go from a squeak to a restrained shout in a second. "It matters if you read something in a newspaper that simply isn't true."

"But not everybody cares about British monarchs or Collins Barracks either, Stephen," I said. "Most people just don't know and don't want to know."

"It still matters," said Stephen. "There are lots of grey areas in newspapers. Features, editorials, things like that. But facts, facts about dates and history aren't like that. A wrong fact is a wrong fact. I just can't help thinking that writing an article without researching your facts properly, well, that's immoral. It's even more immoral if you think you can get away with sloppy research just because people don't care. It's as if you're hiding your ignorance behind everybody else's indifference. That's lazy, or at least it starts out being lazy and ends up immoral."

"You're nodding your head with great vehemence, Antonia," said Grace. "Do you think I started by being lazy and ended up immoral?" Since that was just what I had been thinking, I was struck dumb. "Antonia takes ideas personally, you know, Stephen," she said in this light, biscuity voice. "She's not very interested in abstract ideas." She was being cruel, quite like Grandma, in fact, explaining me to someone else as if I wasn't there, belittling me as if she didn't know me or like me.

"I didn't say anything," I said furiously. "I was just listening to Stephen."

"Well, I must be going," said Stephen grabbing his anorak. "I'll be late if I don't hurry. Do you want me to walk you home, Antonia, or do you want to stay?"

The both turned toward me, Stephen and Grace, and stared at me through the soft, smoky light. I did want to walk home with Stephen and my bike. I wanted, quite urgently, to be with Mum in our safe yellow house and I most certainly did not want to stay with Grace, strange, familiar Grace with the bump and the new spiky manner. Grace who held all my old affection.

"I'll stay," I said because I knew that running away would be worse later.

"Well, see Stephen out. Does he have a bike?" said Grace, who was obviously learning about practicalities in preparation for motherhood. Fuss, fuss.

"No," said Stephen. "I walk and Antonia's left her bike in that mews place where it'll probably get stolen. I'll move it for you if you don't want to come down, Antonia." I did want to come down so we moved my bike from the mews in near silence and left it in the hall and then Stephen did a most surprising thing. He hugged me suddenly and pecked at my hair. Was that a kiss?—or not?

"It'll be all right," he said, "whatever it is. She's very impressive, your aunt but she can't be very happy, can she? I think you were right to stay." Then another quick hug and he almost ran out the front door. I watched him stride down the street. And then he turned around and waved. "I'll see you," he shouted. "We'll go for a walk."

Well, that settled the most troubling of my unasked questions. He'd see me, he said. We'd go for a walk. Poor Aunt Grace. I am not at all keen on counting my blessings in the ordinary way but it's much easier to feel sorry for other people if you're surging with joy.

Grace had left the flat door open and was back in the bentwood chair when I'd puffed happily up the stairs.

"Don't say it again," I said. "I know he's a nice boy. One day someone will murder him because all adults can say about him is that he's a very nice boy."

"And intelligent and interesting," said Aunt Grace with a smile. "Will you stay the night? We could talk."

I stayed. We talked. I can hardly bear to think about it even now. I don't know quite what I'd been expecting. I knew that Brian was a crook and I thought he was stupid and limited and unpleasant as well. But, I'd reasoned, all sorts of perfectly pleasant people fall in love with truly frightful ones. Mum often says that she wishes she could cut most of the couples she know in half. Nices, she says do tend to fall in love with nasties and vice versa. Unfortunately Grace's story wasn't like that at all.

"I was never in love with Brian, you know," said Grace in this bed-time story voice. "I didn't love him. Sometimes I didn't even like him. He was fun in the beginning. Well most people, men that is, are fun in the beginning if they seem to admire you very much and spend a lot of money on you. He behaved as if he was rich. He didn't ever talk very much about himself. I suppose I talked all the time. I talked about the family and about you, you particularly, and about teaching. It was only after a while that I realised that he wasn't listening. It was quite eerie really. 'Antonia,' he'd say. 'Antonia, which is she?' Just after he'd been laughing at some story I'd told him about you."

"Willed amnesia," I said thinking about Grandma.

"Oh much worse than that," said Grace. "His forgetting was as if he'd never known at all. It was, well, weird."

"Eerie," I said helpfully. I wasn't trying to be funny. I just felt as if my voice could keep this story a certain safe distance away. Aunt Grace looked at me sharply.

"Yes, eerie. And then, this is really the worst, Antonia," she stopped as if it really was the worst. "One morning when we were in bed, it was early summer, this was, before I got pregnant, he turned around to me and said 'You're a teacher, right?' as if he didn't know quite who I was. As if there were so many other women and I was just one of them. And then I decided I'd have his baby."

"Pretty odd moment to choose," I muttered. I was almost too horrified to speak.

"Well it wasn't, you know," said Grace "It wasn't at all. He didn't know me. He'd just proved that. And I wanted a baby very much by then. What else could I do? It was all too tacky and too difficult. And Brian had just sort of come along. It was," said Grace, "quite providential."

"Well, if that's your view of providence it certainly isn't mine," I said.

I was disturbed not just by Grace's story but by the way she was telling it. She was still using this slightly sing-song, bed-time story voice, as if she'd been rehearsing this story for a long time and had finally come to believe in it. As if it must be true because she'd recited it to herself so often. The whole thing made my mind start to zing and zang again. It was like one of those dreams when you find something only to lose it again immediately.

"You mean you used Brian, like men use women?'

"Oh don't be so self-righteous, Antonia!" Grace's voice was strong and low and furious, the sing-song had gone. "What on earth do you know about it? I know you're angry with me about Liz—or that's what you want to think you're feeling. But remember that Liz is more than just your mother. She's Liz. She can make choices if she wants to. She's not my victim, you know. She allows herself to be Grandma's."

"Well she's stopped," I said crossly, "and I wasn't comparing you, Aunt Grace."

"Oh yes you were. You know you were. You've been busy turning it into a morality play. Liz is good constant Liz who looks after Grandma and I'm bad Grace who sleeps with a man she doesn't even like. But at least I wanted to sleep with Brian, however questionable or extraordinary that might seem to you. I enjoyed it a lot more than Liz ever enjoyed doing anything for Grandma. There is nothing particularly moral about being nice to Grandma, Antonia. You know that and Liz knows it too. And there's nothing terribly immoral about exploiting Brian. In fact I don't think you *could* exploit Brian or use him either. I didn't like some of the feelings I had about myself when I was with him but I can't say that I mind at all about what I did to Brian. And neither do you. I mean I can just about stomach your protective feelings for Liz but don't ask me to believe that you're truly worried about Brian." Her words danced and dazzled in the still smoky air. She stood up and stretched her body with one hand against the table. I felt a bit dizzy myself.

"These protective feelings you're having for Brian and

Liz are a way of dressing up your revulsion as moral outrage and it won't work, Antonia. That's the sort of thing that Grandma goes in for. And now I'm going to pour myself a glass of wine."

"You shouldn't," I said, "drink when you're pregnant."

Aunt Grace sensibly ignored this piece of bitchery and staggered to the kitchen returning, I was relieved to see, with a glass of wine but no bottle. I wasn't particularly worried about the dear little baby but I did think that Grace was quite angry enough without wine. And why angry for heaven's sake? I was the one who'd been angry with Grace and now the whole thing had changed. I'd felt sensible when I asked her that question about men using women, sensible if a bit unreal, and now she'd made me feel foolish because it was true. Who could exploit Brian and what did it matter if someone actually managed it? And what did I care or know about it? It's disconcerting to find yourself in the wrong when you were quite sure you were in the right and I felt a bit lonely for my anger which was changing into a kind of worried fear.

"The thing is, Grace, that I don't know about it. I don't understand it," I said when she was safely returned to her bentwood chair, glass of pale wine glittering in front of her. "I don't understand it at all. You didn't love Brian. You didn't even like him so why on earth did you decide to have his baby?"

"I can't tell you exactly why," said Aunt Grace crossly, "and if I were you I'd start thinking about my own motives and my own feelings. You might find them to be a little less tidy and predictable than you imagine. Life simply isn't like that. You don't wake up in the morning and stretch and say 'Well here's a man I dislike, I think I'll have his baby.' "

"That's the way you told it," I said. "I can't make sense of it if you don't make sense of it."

"Oh *sense*," said Grace scornfully, taking a sip of her wine. "How much of anyone's emotional life makes *sense*? I did want to get pregnant. And Brian talked about having babies all the time. He said he wanted to marry me and he wanted to have children. He said he had a very high IQ. He sounded as if he wanted to found a dynasty of brilliant children with himself as paterfamilias. But of course that's just what I didn't want. I didn't want to marry him. In fact I've never wanted to marry anybody. I don't think," said Aunt Grace, thoughtfully fingering her wine-glass, "that I've ever met a married woman whom I envied or wanted to be like. I'm not good at compromises and I doubt if I could manage the sheer stickiness of marriage, all those gluey guilt feelings wrapping around your skin. So I didn't want to marry Brian and I didn't want to have his child until that morning when he didn't know who I was. And then I decided that since he didn't know who I was it would be quite safe to have his baby."

""But Grace," I said, "It doesn't make sense." Grace winced at "sense." "All right, I'll leave sense out of it. But you told Mum, when you told her about the baby, you said then that you didn't mean to get pregnant." And I thought of that end-of-summer Sunday which seemed ages long ago.

"It was a long time ago, wasn't it?" said Grace. "I said I didn't quite mean to get pregnant." She smiled at me. It was part of our bond. We both have memories like tape-recorders. Not for useful facts, like the price of rice, but for odd moments of conversation that interest us. In the homesick garden days we used to play a game about who in the family said what and when.

"Well, if you didn't mean to get pregnant, what did you mean? To get almost pregnant?"

"I suppose I left it up to fate," said Grace, "which was, no doubt, highly irresponsible of me. I didn't know if I could get pregnant so I stopped planning not to. Do you know what age I am, Antonia?"

"Older than Mum," I said promptly because it was one of those little facts that Mum tended to mention rather often.

"I'm forty-two and some months," said Grace. "And until last year it never bothered me all that much. I never envied Liz when you were a baby. I didn't like the thought of babies and breast-feeding and nappy-changing any more than I liked the thought of marriage. In fact I thought babies and marriage were the same sort of thing. I thought nature didn't intend me to have a baby. When you grew up I got to like you, love you but I never thought of you as a daughter. You were a person to me."

"I know," I said. That was why I'd always trusted Grace.

"But then last year I went to see an ex-pupil of mine after she'd had a baby. She was at home and she asked me to hold the baby. I wouldn't have touched it in hospital. In hospital, I'd have had more, well more of what you'd call sense, than to hold a baby," said Grace, "But I picked this baby up. He had red down on his head and he was all wrinkly and shut-eyed and he moved his little hands about as if he was swimming."

"Babies are like that," I said.

"The last time I saw you with a baby, you looked as if you wanted to drop it," said Aunt Grace briskly. "I must say

I've felt like that myself. But this time I wanted to hug the baby and squeeze him and oh, just have it for my own. And after that I'd wake up in the night and think about the rest of my life and never, ever, having a baby and then Brian came and kept on talking about babies. I didn't love him or even like him enough to have his baby if he was going to be around but after that morning I realised that he wouldn't be around much longer so I sort of left it up to fate."

I didn't say anything for a while. Aunt Grace seemed quite content to sit there staring at her empty wine-glass while I thought about babies and revulsion. I don't like babies myself. I've always thought, felt, hoped, that all that yearning over them was a bit false. I mean, if there is a maternal instinct why don't I feel something when I look at those red, angry, little faces? I baby-sat for a friend of Mum's once and the baby yelled and yelled from the minute its parents went out the door. I fed that baby and it pushed away the teat of its bottle. I changed it (it was a boy) and it squirted at my favourite blouse. I walked it and tried to cuddle it and it just screamed and screamed. I did make an attempt to summon up some maternal feelings for the wretched little brat but they just wouldn't come. Eventually I had to put it back in its cot because, if I'd held it one more minute, I'd have been tempted to turn it upside down and slap it. I hadn't liked my feelings about that ghastly baby but I'd thought that perhaps it wasn't so dreadful to have no maternal instinct because of Grace. She'd never shown any signs of maternal instinct either and she seemed to have survived as a complete and lovely person without it. I'd never told her about the baby-sitting or the terrible rage that that baby had made me feel but I'd always felt that if I did tell Grace, then Grace would understand.

And now Grace had changed. There she was yearning away just like all the other women in the world. So many changes. I thought at that moment that I'd have an image of Brian and Grace in bed in the morning for the rest of my life. Strangers in the Sack. There was something about it that was much more obscene than any pornography (not much) that I could possibly imagine. I giggled and my giggle squeaked around the room as Grace gazed at me in astonishment. Strangers in the Sack indeed.

"I'm sorry," I said. "Just something silly I was thinking. I'm really sorry." And I was. I hated this vision I was having of Grace. Brian's Grace, the baby's Grace, this figure in a horrible, rapid strip-cartoon that had started to track across my mind. This figure who really wasn't Grace. My Grace.

"It's just that you seem to have changed so much. I mean it's not like you."

"Oh God, Antonia, from the beginning of time one person has been telling another person that that's not like you when what he or she really means is that that's not *my* idea of you. What do you know about me, about how I am, when you're not looking?"

She stood up rapidly and touched her back in that way that pregnant women do in films and started moving jerkily around the room. But she wasn't pitiable or even touching. Her steps thumped down the threadbare carpet and she stumbled slightly against the rugs as she weaved backwards and forwards across the room.

"It's not just that you're a prig." The mirrors in her dress sparkled as she moved. "It's worse than that. You *want* to be a prig. It's not that you can't understand that I might be attracted to a man I didn't like. It's that you don't want to understand. You're building a tiny house of sex-free sense for yourself and it'll box you in the end, if you're not careful. You'll have to keep all the interesting people out and the dull ones in. I know, I know," she said waving her hand at me although I wasn't trying to say anything, "rules are very comforting things to have at your age but rules are there for people, not people for rules. You always used to understand that even when you thought I should be providing breakfast for you. Do you remember? 'Children need breakfast' you said that first time you came to stay...But you were a very accommodating little girl...then.. You wanted a mother but you accepted an aunt, sardine sandwiches, take-aways and all. And now, I think, you're twisting your instincts...If Aunt Grace doesn't fit into your rules, then ditch Aunt Grace but not the rules. Rules make sense because they keep away fear and people can't do that for you. Why are you laughing, Antonia?"

I didn't know. A curious nervous bubble had started to balloon under my diaphragm as Aunt Grace tripped around the room, hair flying, mirrors trembling and twinkling. It was relief, joy, fury.

"I'm laughing because I'm so angry," I said. "I'd want to hit you otherwise. And you should see yourself dancing about. Slow, slow, prig, prig, slow."

Aunt Grace subsided on the bentwood chair and grinned. "You are a prig, Antonia. And now you must go to bed."

And then it was all blankets and sag-bags and cushions and would I be comfortable on the floor.

When I was nestled safely in my cocoon on the floor with blankets cosily covering me, I looked up and found Aunt Grace looking down. It wasn't a tender, yearning or maternal look. Grace's face was sad, all drawn down under a ferocious frown. She always looks ferocious when she's sad.

"I wish I thought you understood what I was saying," she said.

"Who can see into the mind of another?" I said, trying to sound sleepy. I didn't know if I did understand it or not and I was still very cross because it isn't pleasant being called a prig, particularly if you think it might be true. I mean I thought I might think about what Grace had said, later, but I didn't want her watching me while I was thinking it.

"You should go to bed too, Aunt Grace," I said. "It's not a good idea doing without your sleep when you're pregnant."

"Prig," said Grace smiling.

"Yes, well," I said. "Give a dog a bad name and it'll bite."

I couldn't sleep. Aunt Grace used to say that she thought I had rubber limbs because I could collapse on any surface, however hard, and sleep till morning. You could say that sleep is one of my major talents. But the floor was uncomfortable and my limbs had started to ache seriously by the time I heard a church bell strike, one, two, three, four. Church bells in the night sound a kind of mysterious comfort. Comfort, prig, puritanical, instincts. How could you twist your own instincts? I always thought that instincts were things you had or didn't have—like my maternal one. Nature was in charge of them and could give or withold them. But this was the first I'd heard of free will in the matter of instincts. But perhaps it was a bit like forgetting and remembering. I once forgot something seriously and vitally important, a message for Mum or Dad, and Mum yelled at me.

"How *could* you have forgotten!" she shouted.

"I didn't mean to forget," I said. "It just happened."

"Nothing just happens," said Mum. "You do things."

So maybe I could ask Mum about this business with instincts. Maybe, on the other hand, I wouldn't. But at least I was back with Grace and Grace was her furious funny self once more.

🐛🐛🐛

CHAPTER ELEVEN

As it happened I needn't have bothered about wondering whether I should talk to Mum or not. Mum it was who talked to me. She was standing on the top of the stepladder when I came in from school. She had a bucket attached to a bent wire coat-hanger—one of Dad's nattier little inspirations—and she was washing walls and listening to the radio. Mum washes walls when she wants to think and she reserves the kitchen walls for special occasions because, as she says, you can't wash a bit of kitchen wall. You have to wash all the walls and probably the ceiling as well because the clean bits make the dirty bits look even dirtier. So I knew that Mum was feeling like thinking about something important for a particularly long time when I saw her in the kitchen.

"I heard from Grace, Antonia," said Mum as I put my schoolbag down on the kitchen floor. "And take that bag out of here and put it in your room."

When I came back she was sliding a dishcloth across the wet wall. No point in washing, she says, without drying. Always complete your actions, Antonia.

"Grace phoned me," said Mum, stretching her body at right angles to the ladder to reach a distant sud.

"Mum, move the ladder!" Mum quite often stretches herself on the floor while she's washing walls. She hates getting down from the ladder and moving it. She'd prefer to perform personal acrobatics and she's always forgetting to adjust Dad's patent ladder hinge (another clothes hanger) so that the ladder separates and falls flat on its face and Mum with it.

"Oh all right," said Mum and got down, moved the ladder and got up again. I realised that she didn't want to look at me, or have me feeling as if she was looking at me, while she talked.

"Grace was angry with me," said Mum. "She said I was evasive and inhibited. She roared at me," said Mum wonderingly, "and I roared back."

I was amazed. Mum's not given to roaring. She usually trembles and puts down the phone or walks out the door whenever anybody is cross with her.

"I said that I might be inhibited and evasive but at least I had enough good taste not to sleep with a sleaze-bag like Brian. And then she started to yell at me about good taste and cosy domesticity. She said I was hiding in a bolt-hole of fear."

"Bolt-hole of fear?" I said. "Did Grace really say that?"

"She did," said Mum grimly, removing a cobweb with a sponge, "and it made me very angry. Then she reminded me of something. It was when I was eighteen. I was just about to leave school. Grace was twenty. She was seeing this man. He was a lot older than she was. He had a car. She was out till all hours with him. There used to be terrible rows with Grandma."

Curious, I thought, as I watched Mum jerking about on her ladder, how Grace and Mum could never call Grandma "Mother." I wondered what they'd done before I was born. Not call her anything at all, probably. Perhaps they didn't mention her.

"Anyway," said Mum, "one day Grace said something

that made me think she was sleeping with this man. So I asked her was she. The worst thing was that I didn't want to know. Or at least I wanted to be reassured that she wasn't sleeping with him. And then she said of course she was sleeping with him. What century did I think we were living in for heaven's sake. People talked like that in the Sixties," said Mum as if they didn't talk like that now.

"When she said that I was sick. I went into the bathroom and vomited. I can still see the maker's name on the toilet bowl. Trent Washdown, it was. It was quite an old toilet. That was before Castleknock," said Mum as if the toilet and its age were of vital importance to the story.

"It was as if some horrible insect had crawled into the room we shared and made it all dirty. It was slimy somehow. It never occurred to me at the time that there was something wrong with me. I just thought there was something very wrong with Grace. Grace reminded me about that on the phone," said Mum, climbing down off the step-ladder. She sat down at the kitchen table and lit a cigarette.

"She said I'd made her feel terrible then. I never knew that, you know, Antonia. I was so sorry for myself at the time that I couldn't see Grace. Also I've never been able to believe that what I feel has any effect on anyone. At least I hope it doesn't. But obviously the way I am," said Mum, as if the way she was was some deadly condition, "is having some effect on you. Grace said that when she talked to you the other night about Brian and the baby, she kept on seeing my eighteen-year-old face, sick and revolted."

"Well, I think that was very interfering of her," I said. I mean how could I grow up and untwist my instincts if every conversation I had was going to be monitored by a committee of two. I'd lose my natural spontaneity, that way. Not that I have much natural spontaneity, but if I did have, I'd lose it.

"I don't think it was interference." Mum stubbed out her cigarette and unhooked the bucket, which she emptied in the sink. She turned on the tap and over the rush of water she said, "She wasn't trying to tell tales on you. She was trying to warn me." Mum climbed back up the ladder again with her full bucket and made a great business of rehooking it. Swish, swish went the sponge across the kitchen wall.

"It's all about something that happened a long time ago. I project feelings I want to forget about. Horrible word, project," said Mum thoughtfully, "but very useful too. It's a story really, so I'll begin at the beginning and go on to the end.

"This story starts in Howth, which is where Grandma and Grandpa lived with their two children, Grace and Liz."

"Before Castleknock," I said, entering into the bed-time spirit.

"Before Castleknock," agreed Mum. "Castleknock, well I think Castleknock killed Dad. He couldn't stomach it. Howth was all right. It was an old house near the village in a terrace looking over the sea and though there was a lot of pink about, Grandma saw to that, it wasn't Castleknock. I think we were all reasonably happy in a disappointed sort of way in Howth. Dad was rather silent and patient and absent and Grandma, well you know what Grandma is. She wasn't much better then. But at least Dad was there. He didn't exactly restrain Grandma but I think Grace and I thought he could restrain her if she really went too far. We never decided what too far would be. And perhaps Dad was a coward like me," said Mum viciously as she started with a swoop and a stretch on the kitchen ceiling. I knew she wouldn't be able to resist it. She'd been edging around it for ages.

"Or perhaps she just wore him out. She's always behaved like a tired woman but her will is implacable. She used to rest every afternoon if she could and I always believed that she wound up her malice lying on her bed in the afternoons.

"Anyway Grandma insisted that we shouldn't play with the wrong sort of children so she cultivated the right sort of people. Her taste in people was rather worse than her taste in houses. She fell in love, there's no other word for it, it was a kind of love, with this ghastly English ex-pat sort of family who'd exhausted the Empire. They'd been in Africa somewhere and the African had thrown them out. That's what Reg, the father, used to say. 'The African threw us out.' It gave me," said Mum dreamily," a special sense of affinity with the Mau Mau. I'd heard they were pretty good at throwing people like Reg out.

"They were called Thompson, this family, Reg and Ursula and their sweet children, Quentin and Phyllis."

"He can't have been called Quentin," I said.

"Oh he was," said Mum. "Ursula had ambitions and Quentin was supposed to be clever like Uncle Quentin in *The Famous Five*. They lived in this big brash bungalow near the top of Howth Hill. It had an odd sort of roof, a bit like a pagoda, with turned up corners. Perhaps they were thinking of coolies or something, and it had a porch with stripes and a ding-dong bell."

"Like Grandma's in Castleknock," I said.

"Quite like," said Mum, "In fact I think that's why Grandma bought Castleknock. It reminded her so much of the dear Thompsons.

"Phyllis was Grace's age. She had long black plaits and a smooth, shiny face. She wore smocked dresses and her knee-socks were held up with plaid garters. And she had braces on her teeth. She was very impressive, Phyllis was, and naturally enough after a campaign of afternoon teas by Grandma and Ursula, Phyllis and Grace became inseparable. They used to walk around with their arms around each other. They swopped dolls and glass animals and they spent every minute they could together. The only problem was that I had to come too. Grace and Phyllis didn't want me. Ursula didn't want me. Well, Ursula knew that Grandma was using her as a built-in baby-sitter. She didn't mind Grace because Grace kept Phyllis happy. But she didn't want me. You know, Antonia, the extraordinary thing about women of that generation was how little they liked their children. It was if children interfered with the proper business of motherhood which was cooking and cleaning and keeping the house nice." Mum paused and contemplated the lamp-shade. She'd been washing and wiping and stretching all this time.

"Antonia, do you think I could wash this shade *in situ*, as it were. Without taking it down?"

"No, Mum, you'll electrocute yourself if you do. Go on with the story."

"Well, on Wednesdays and on Saturdays off we went to the Thompsons so that Grandma could have her sacred rest undisturbed by the sound of childish voices. Quentin was always there hanging about. He didn't seem to have any friends. I wondered afterwards if he was slightly retarded. He didn't *look* retarded, mind you. Fine figure of a little brute he was. He was fourteen. I was seven. Grace and Phyllis were nine. Quentin was very handsome, I suppose, in an Aryan, Midwich Cuckoo sort of way. He had bright blue eyes and they blazed.

"Grace and Phyllis used to go for walks and they'd leave me behind in what Ursula called the lounge. Ursula was always in the kitchen baking. She was a mean woman. She'd bake and bake but she'd never give us baked things. Reg was in the biscuit business, I think he was the rep for some English company so Ursula would just open a tin of biscuits for us. Horrible biscuits they were too. They were usually slightly stale.

"So I was left with Quentin in that ghastly lounge with china animals marching in a neat parade in front of the venetian blind. The Thompsons had the first venetian blinds I'd ever seen. After a few visits Quentin started to call me over to his armchair, to read to me he said. I suppose he must have read to me. I can still see the book in his hands. But after a while I realised that he was stroking me, pinching me, rubbing against me. And then he started to make me do things."

"Oh Mum."

"It was terrible because life went on being normal. Ursula went on baking furiously in the kitchen. Grace and Phyllis went on walking the windy, purple, tarmacadam roads in their crisp little dresses and their bright bows. And it was terrible because I was so frightened of it," said Mum coming slowly down the step-ladder.

"I was so frightened of it that I kept on forgetting about it. Until the next time. That wasn't easy because he was always there, everywhere. Grandma got to like him and started to invite him to our house. The boy she always wanted, she said. She adored him. She said it was very unusual for such a great big grown boy to take such an interest in little girls. It was unusual all right," said Mum sitting down at the kitchen table and lighting another cigarette. "And she used to say that she felt quite safe leaving us in his hands. He had very ugly hands."

I moved my chair around the kitchen table closer to Mum. She was shaking and puffing furiously.

"Did you get over it?" It sounded a fairly fatuous question when I'd asked it. After all she wouldn't be sitting there shaking if she'd got over it. She wouldn't have told me if she'd got over it.

Mum looked up at me and smiled.

"I thought I had. I thought I did. Maybe I'd have got over it, really over it, if I hadn't trivialised it, made some sort of wrong sense of it, if I'd tried to remember it more often. But I sliced it off, put it in a separate compartment in my mind and whenever I remembered, which wasn't, oddly enough, that often, I kept on telling myself that nothing really happened. That it wasn't rape, for heaven's sake. That it was just adolescent fooling around."

"But Mum, you were only seven. He was an adolescent. You weren't."

"Yes," said Mum. "I can see that now. I think I've known it for ages really. But I've spent so much of my life thumping that time down as if," said Mum gazing up at her gleaming ceiling, "as if it were yeast dough. Ursula used to make yeast bread. It had this strange, warm smell and she'd make it in a big plastic bowl. It used to swell up and she'd thump it down but each time she thumped it down it would swell up again and stick to her fingers."

We sat there close and quiet in the damp kitchen. After a while I asked Mum if Quentin had, well, molested Grace. Mum said he hadn't and, while I was wondering how she knew, Mum said she knew because she'd asked Grace—much later—if Quentin had ever tried to touch her.

"And Grace said that he had tried but she'd slapped his face. It's funny," said Mum sadly, "I never thought of that. And when Grace asked if he'd touched me I said no. It was much later then. The Thompsons had gone home to 'back Britain' by then. Far too late. But anyway I said no. It seemed safer to say no."

I wondered if Grace had believed Mum. After all you don't trip about asking questions about boys touching girls if you haven't a special reason for it. Had Grace really escaped Quentin? Probably, I thought, when I remembered about her boyfriend and his car and when I thought about Grace being Grace and Mum being Mum.

It should have been a shock, what Mum had told me. Enough to put me off sex for life. But it wasn't like that at all. Maybe it's different, seeing something nasty in somebody else's woodshed. It was terrible and sad but not shocking somehow. Not unexpected anyway. It wasn't a leaping-out-at-you secret. It was something that had been there all along. Something waiting to be told and now that it was told I felt a strange sort of relief. And Mum, I think Mum felt it too.

❦❦❦

CHAPTER TWELVE

I wish I could say that everything changed, changed utterly, after Mum's revelations and that a terrible beauty was born. But Mum is still Mum. She will always, I think, shake and tremble whenever anyone is cross with her. She'll always cringe and flinch and she'll always try not to. She made it up with Grandma. Grandma went into an expensive old people's home because, she said, "hired help is not what it was." By "hired help" she meant the agency nurse. So Mum visits her in the home where Grandma terrorises all the other old ladies—and flirts, ever so delicately, with the old men. But Grandma doesn't come to our house any more. Mum told her that she was too frail to travel. Typical Mum. And Grandma was so pleased about that that she sent Mum out immediately to buy her a walking stick which she now uses to rap at the legs of anyone who isn't paying attention to her. Anyone within reach, that is. Grandma complains that the nurses are "very neglectful."

Grace had her baby which was very large, ten pounds, Mum said. It was, is, a girl and Mum visits Grace almost as often as she visits Grandma and yearns over it, in a slightly shamefaced way. Dad lost interest when he heard the baby was a girl. If it had been a boy he wanted it to be called Balthazar but he didn't have any ambitions about girl's names. Grace called the baby, who is very fat, singularly unattractive and red-cheeked, Isabelle. Dad says she doesn't look like an Isabelle.

"Isabelle is a dainty name," he said.

"What name does she look like?" asked Mum.

"Oh, something solemn and fat," said Dad. "Euphemia or Honoria."

Grace is leaving the flat and moving into a house in the suburbs. She's also buying a car. Mum, for all her yearning, was quite horrified by these developments.

"You can't live in the suburbs. You can't buy a house on a new estate," she said. "Those houses are made of cardboard. And a car..." Mum thinks that cars are the ultimate expression of human decadence.

"Well, plenty of people do," said Grace, who was sitting at our kitchen table nursing the baby. "Plenty of people do. I can't stay in the flat with the baby because the landlord doesn't like babies and he won't do repairs and the plumbing, which was quite amusing when I was on my own, isn't at all amusing now. I can't afford an old house near the city because they won't give me a mortgage for it and even if they did I don't have the time or the ingenuity to transform it into something practical. So I need a house in the suburbs and the house in the suburbs needs a car."

"But you can't drive!" wailed Mum.

"No," said Grace, "but I'll learn."

She's learning and Mum looks after Isabelle while Grace goes on her driving lessons. Which means, of course, that when Mum visits Grandma during the driving lessons, I get to look after Isabelle, who is now six months old and has taken to smiling at me.

"Silly baby," I told her the other day. "Don't you know I hate babies?" Clearly Isabelle didn't know because she went right on smiling. She even gurgled at me, a sound that was almost a laugh. I'm not about to yearn over Isabelle,

God forbid, but I'm beginning to understand how the species survives. Isabelle looks quite credible when she smiles.

As for Stephen, I think I'll be an old, old woman before he does more than hold my hand in public and he'll be an older man before I reach out and touch him. But we do go for walks and these days I leave my bicycle behind. We walk along, shoulder to shoulder, and sometimes he squeezes my arm to call attention to some particularly attractive or deplorable architectural feature. Sometimes he gives me a quick hug goodbye. Yesterday I pulled a leaf out of his hair and he smiled at me and stood there, very still, looking at me. But I moved away very quickly and squeezed the leaf into the palm of my hand. He said nothing and I'm meeting him tomorrow. Next time I'll try to stay still.